Steel and Sacrifice

Shirley Montague

Contents

Chapter 1

Patroklos' arms were drenched in blood, the warm and sticky liquid coating his skin and clothes. He looked down to see a lifeless body lying beneath him, both a friend and a stark reminder of the violence and death that surrounded him. He had seen his fair share of tragedy and loss, but nothing could have prepared him for the horrors of this war.

The battlefield was a scene of chaos and destruction, with thousands of soldiers lying dead or dying all around him. The air was thick with the stench of death, and the sounds of battle echoed in his ears.

Despite the overwhelming sense of despair and hopelessness, Patroklos knew that he had to act. He couldn't just sit there and watch as more and more soldiers fell to their deaths. He had a duty to help those who were still alive, to do everything in his power to save as many lives as possible.

The days had been unseasonably warm, the sun beating down on us with a fierce intensity that left us feeling sweaty and uncomfortable. But then there was the boy with the golden hair, and his touch was like a cool breeze on a sweltering day.

We sat in the shade of an old ambrosia tree, his fingers moving gently over mine. He was teaching me how to strum the strings of his lyre as he hummed a soothing melody. The melody he hummed was a gentle, soothing tune that filled the air around us with a sense of peace and calm. His eyes were closed, his face serene as he lost himself in the music, and I could feel myself being swept away by the magic of the moment.

His hair, a bright and shining halo of gold, caught the light of the sun and shimmered like a thousand tiny stars. It was a sight to behold, one that drew the eyes and held them captive.

Once he finished his lullaby, he opened his eyes, and I was struck by their beauty. They were the colour of the ocean with little spots of green, like tiny islands amidst a vast sea. Not many people noticed them except for those who were allowed to be as close to him as I was in this moment. I was so close to him, in fact, that I could feel the warmth of his breath brush against my skin.

"What are you thinking about?" He asked, now fully looking at me.

"Just you, Achilles." I replied.

"Is that all?" He question with a sympathetic grin. I knew what he was insinuating.

"Dad...it's his birthday today." My father had died a long time ago fighting in battle.

Our fathers were the closest of friends, and we spent our childhood together, learning from their example and becoming just like them. Our bond grew stronger with each passing day, and we were inseparable.

However, when my father passed away, my world was turned upside down. It was then that Achilles' father, Peleus, stepped in and took me under his wing. He treated me as if I were his own son, and I was grateful for his kindness and generosity.

Peleus was a revered king known for his fierce leadership and unwavering loyalty. Despite ruling over a relatively small kingdom, his kingdom was highly respected due to the Myrmidons, his fearless and disciplined warriors.

Their weaponry was also considered the most advanced within the Greek world. While other rulers conquered and celebrated, Peleus instead directed his efforts towards transforming his people into an unbeatable army, equipped with weapons that surpassed those of any adversary.

"Do you still miss him?" Achilles asked.

"Every day." I replied earnestly. "But every time his birthday comes, it's just...harder."

"You know... he was a great man and a greater warrior. I don't remember much of him but, Father, said he was the best he had." Achilles spoke with a sense of reverence and deep admiration.

"I know he was." Everyone would tell me how great he was and that him dying in battle was the most honourable death anyone could ask for. To me, it didn't matter. In the end, he was buried in the ground like any other man, and he was gone from my life. "But what difference does it make when he's gone from my life?"

"He died a warriors death. There is nothing better than that in this world."

Achilles rose to his feet, he stretched his arms and legs, feeling the tightness of his muscles loosen under the warmth of the sun as its rays of light danced across his face.

"Is that all life's about? Being the greatest warrior?" I asked with slight contempt in my voice.

"It's all it needs to be."

I hated it when he talked like this. When he talked about battle and the glory it comes with it. I knew there was more to him than just a warrior. He possessed a melodious voice that was almost angelic, and his musical prowess was truly remarkable. On top of that, he was an exceptional athlete, with the potential to compete in various athletic competitions. It was disheartening to think that he could channel his talents towards something constructive, rather than using them to take lives.

The day unfolded in a typical manner after that as we indulged in a sumptuous spread of delectable foods and drinks. We then proceeded to engage in vigorous training sessions, striving to hone our combat skills to perfection, in which of course Achilles was always the victor. Finally, we devoted the remaining hours to immersing ourselves in scholarly pursuits before retiring for the night.

"Are you asleep?" Achilles whispered.

Last year, when Achilles turned 13, he was faced with the important decision of selecting a companion to accompany him for the rest of his life. As his best friend, he chose me, and I readily accepted. My decision was driven by a sense of obligation to his father, who had taken me in and by my desire to safeguard my dearest friend. I was determined to ensure his safety, come what may.

Ever since that fateful day, I have remained unwaveringly by Achilles' side. My entire existence revolving around his. From the moment I rise in the morning to the times when I eat, train, and even sleep, my thoughts are consumed with his well-being. I have made it my life's mission to protect and serve him, and I do so with unwavering loyalty and dedication.

"No, I can't sleep." I replied.

"What's on your mind?" He rose from his king-sized bed and made his way towards my comparatively smaller one.

At times, I couldn't help but feel a twinge of envy towards the sheer size of Achilles' bed. Although mine was comfortable enough, I had to admit that his bed was a sight to behold. Despite his repeated offers to share his bed with me, I always declined with grace. Deep down, I knew that Achilles was only trying to be kind, but it wasn't right for a royal of his stature to share his bed with someone of lower rank. I was grateful for his generosity, but I also knew my place in the hierarchy and didn't want to overstep my bounds.

"Nothing important," I replied nonchalantly, trying to hide the thoughts racing through my mind.

"Come on, everything in that mind of yours is important." He complimented me, and I couldn't help but feel a sense of pride wash over me. A small grin threatened to form on my lips, but I turned away so that he wouldn't see it. I knew that if he caught a glimpse of it, he would tease me mercilessly, and I wasn't in the mood for that right now.

Out of nowhere, I felt his weight press against me as he wrapped his arm around my torso. I could feel him squeezing himself into my bed, and I knew that he must have been lying in an awkward position. It was clear that he was trying to get comfortable, but I couldn't help but feel a little uncomfortable myself.

"What are you doing?" I asked, feeling confused by his sudden intrusion.

"Every time I offer my bed to you, you refuse me. So, I wanted to see why yours is apparently so much better than mine." He explained, his voice tinged with a hint of playfulness. I could feel his breath on my neck as he spoke, and it sent shivers down my spine. Despite my initial confusion, I couldn't help but feel a sense of amusement at his antics.

"Hmm, it's actually not bad. I might start sleeping here from now on." He continued, shuffling around in an attempt not to fall off the bed.

I couldn't help but smile at his playful behaviour, but I quickly buried my face into the softness of my pillow in an attempt to silence my chuckles. As much as I enjoyed his antics, I also didn't want to encourage them at this late hour.

After a few moments, I noticed his breathing gradually slowing down. Yet, I could still feel the soft rhythm of his breaths caressing the skin of my neck and the steady thump of his heart beating against my back. The warmth of his body against mine filled me with a sense of comfort and security, making me feel safe and content in the stillness of the night.

In a calm and measured tone, he apologized for the earlier incident, "I'm sorry about earlier today. I didn't mean to upset you." His slow and steady breaths filled the room, creating a sense of tranquillity. He acknowledged my aversion to violence and the pain I had endured through the loss of my father. However, he also emphasized the honour and purpose that came with being a warrior, including eternal fame. "Fighting and dying as a warrior means something. It's glorious and gives our lives purpose." His words were sincere and heartfelt, but the pain of my loss still lingered, making it difficult to fully accept his perspective.

I turned around to face him, his face only inches away from mine. As I spoke, I tried to convey the depth of my feelings. "I understand what you mean," I said, "but if I had to choose between my father being dead and famous or alive and a nobody, then I would choose the latter" My heart ached as I acknowledged the pain of his absence. "Because, to me, he would still be someone." I searched his eyes, hoping he would understand the depth of my emotions and see that there was more to life than glory and fame.

"I...I guess I understand," he said hesitantly, "I just don't agree."

I could sense his discomfort, but I wanted him to know that our disagreement didn't change how much I valued our relationship. "It's okay," I reassured him, "we don't have to agree on everything, or even anything at all. I will always stand by your side, no matter what." My voice was soft and gentle, conveying the depth of my commitment. "Even if we disagree on something, I will never let it destroy the bond we have." I held his gaze, hoping he could see the sincerity in my eyes and feel the warmth of my words.

As I finished speaking, he broke into a smile, and I couldn't help but smile back. "Now, can you please leave my bed?" I quipped, trying to lighten the mood, "I'm getting squeezed against the wall."

Achilles laughed but made no move to leave. "Absolutely not!" he replied, a mischievous glint in his eyes, "I just got comfortable." He shifted slightly, making himself even more at home.

Chapter 2

The heat of the sun was almost unbearable, making us gasp for breath as we fought. Beads of sweat dripped down our bare chests, glistening in the sunlight, and the sound of our spears collided with a resounding clash.

Achilles gripped the golden spear with a fierce intensity, his knuckles turning white as he felt the weight of the weapon in his hand. The spear was a thing of beauty, crafted by none other than Hephaestus himself, the greatest blacksmith in all of Greece. Its metal surface gleamed in the sunlight, a testament to the skill and artistry of its maker.

But there was something else about the spear that made it even more special. It seemed to hum with a strange energy, as if it had a life of its own. Achilles mentioned he could feel the power coursing through it, as if it were alive and eager to be used.

Hephaestus, the legendary blacksmith of the Greek world, was renowned for his unparalleled craftsmanship. His skill with metal was unmatched, and his creations were coveted by all who desired the finest weapons and armour. Sadly, the great Hephaestus had passed away less than a decade ago, leaving a void in the world of blacksmithing that no one had been able to fill.

Peleus and Hephaestus had been close friends for many years, and the blacksmith held a deep respect for the king. As a token of this friendship, Hephaestus created a weapon for Peleus' son, Achilles - the deadliest weapon he had ever crafted. And it was also his last.

This act of generosity was a testament to the bond between Hephaestus and Peleus, and it spoke volumes about the blacksmith's character. Though he was gone, his legacy would live on within his creation.

Achilles stood before me, his posture relaxed and at ease, as if he were waiting for a friend to arrive. I couldn't help but feel a sense of frustration at his nonchalance. We both knew that I was no match for him in combat, yet he seemed to relish in his superiority, flaunting it with every move.

"Come on! Attack me already!" Achilles' face beamed with a smile as he taunted me to attack. His confidence was palpable, and it only served to fuel my own frustration.

"Can you stop?!" I charged at him furiously with my silver spear, feeling the weight of my inferior weapon in comparison to his bulkier, more ornate one.

As I lunged forward, I couldn't help but feel a sense of inadequacy. My spear lacked the intricate engravings that adorned Achilles', making it little more than a functional weapon compared to his work of art.

Despite my efforts, Achilles continued to toy with me, dodging my attacks with ease and taunting me with his superior skills.

"Stop, what?" He asked, feigning cluelessness as he continued to taunt me. His words only served to fuel my frustration, and I felt my anger boiling over.

Agitated with both him and myself, I threw my weight towards Achilles, thrusting my spear with all my might.

But Achilles was too quick, too skilled. With a deft sidestep, he evaded my attack, leaving me off-balance and vulnerable. In one swift motion, he used his superior strength to bump me to the ground, leaving me reeling and disoriented.

The hot sand beneath me seared my skin, sending waves of discomfort through my body. But in that moment, I was too consumed by my frustration to care. I had been bested by Achilles, and the sting of defeat was all I could feel.

With a determined effort, I pushed myself to my feet, coughing and sputtering as I tried to clear the sand from my mouth. My body was slick with sweat, and I could feel the grains of sand sticking to my skin, grinding against me with each movement.

My voice rose to a shout as I confronted him, my frustration boiling over into a torrent of anger. "Why do you always have to do that? Why do you have to act like you're better than me?" I demanded, my words ringing out across the empty beach.

Achilles stood before me, his expression calm and collected, as if he had been expecting this outburst. "Because I am better," he replied matter-of-factly. "You will never learn if I always go easy on you."

I knew he was right, of course. If he went easy on me, I would never improve, never learn from my mistakes. But even as I grudgingly acknowledged this fact, my anger still simmered beneath the surface, a seething mix of frustration and resentment.

"Boys! That's enough practise!" King Peleus' voice carried across the beach from the path that led to the palace. It rang out with a commanding authority that brooked no argument. "It's time to eat."

Without a word, we moved to sheath our spears, each of us reaching for the small button that would cause the weapon to shrink down to the size of a relay baton. The air was thick with the sound of metal on metal, the soft hiss of air escaping from the shrinking weapons, and the rustle of cloth as we secured them to our belts.

As we trudged up the path to the palace, I could feel the heat of the day bearing down on me, the sweat mingling with the sand and sticking to my skin in an uncomfortable, gritty layer. The air was thick with the smell of salt and sea, and I longed for the cool relief of the palace's shaded courtyards.

But as we reached the top of the hill, my thoughts were interrupted by the sound of King Peleus's voice, ringing out with authority. "Care to explain why you were training at the beach after I've told you not to?" he demanded, his posture tall and authoritative. "We have training grounds for a reason, and if either of you gets hurts there'll be help nearby."

"Sorry, Dad, but training always gets us so sweaty. We just like to go for a swim right away after we're done." Achilles explained to his father.

Peleus regarded us both for a moment, his blue eyes scanning our sweat-soaked bodies with a critical eye. "Hmm," Peleus murmured, his voice low and thoughtful. "You both are indeed a mess," he continued, a hint of amusement creeping into his tone. "But still, next time, do bring someone else with you. I dont want either of you getting hurt or worse." He concluded, a smile spreading across his face as he ruffled our hair in a show of affection.

After getting cleaned up, we entered the grand dining halls of the palace, the first thing that struck us was the stark contrast between the scorching heat outside and the coolness that enveloped us within. The marbled floors, with their smooth and polished surface, seemed to exude a refreshing aura that instantly calmed our senses.

At the head of the table sat King Peleus, the patriarch of the family, his regal presence commanding respect and awe. To his right sat Achilles, his valiant son, who exuded an air of confidence and strength. And beside him sat me, chosen by Achilles as his trusted companion and confidante.

As we settled in, the absence of the Queen was palpable, a familiar void that had become a regular occurrence. The grandeur of the dining halls seemed to diminish in her absence, as if her presence was the missing piece that completed the puzzle of the royal family.

Queen Thetis was a woman of deep faith and devotion, spending much of her time in the grand temple of Poseidon. The temple was a sight to behold, with its towering columns and intricate carvings that spoke of a time long past. The sound of waves crashing against the shore added to the mystical atmosphere of the place, as if the God of the sea himself was present.

The Olympians had proven time and again that they were willing to help those in need. And for Queen Thetis, her unwavering faith in Poseidon and the other Gods gave her strength and comfort in a world that was often unpredictable and unforgiving.

Suddenly, the doors burst open, and a hush fell over the room as all of us turned to the figure who had just entered. It was the Queen herself, a regal and imposing presence that commanded respect and admiration.

The Queen's visits were rare, and her unexpected appearance sent a ripple of excitement through the room. King Peleus, her beloved husband, was the first to rise from his chair, a look of pure joy on his face.

"My love!" he exclaimed, his voice ringing out across the hall. "You are here! How wonderful!"

As she approached King Peleus and Achilles, her face lit up with a radiant smile that seemed to brighten the entire room.

"Hello, my loves!" she exclaimed, her voice ringing out with a joyous lilt. To my surprise, Achilles had made his way to her side and was embracing her with all his strength, his face contorted with emotion.

"Mom! I missed you!" he moaned, his voice thick with tears. The sight of the soon to be great warrior weeping openly in the arms of his mother was a testament to the strength of their bond, and it was clear that the Queen's love for her son was unwavering and unconditional.

It had been so long since I had seen Queen Thetis that I could barely recall the last time she had graced us with her presence. Perhaps it was two or three years ago.

As I watched her now, greeting King Peleus and Achilles with open arms, I couldn't help but feel a sense of awe at her regal bearing and commanding presence. She was a woman of great power and grace, and her beauty was matched only by her strength and resilience.

The Queen's voice was soft and gentle as she cupped Achilles' face in her hands, studying his features with a mother's loving gaze. "I missed you too, my little soldier," she murmured, a tender smile playing at the corners of her lips. "Oh, how handsome you've grown."

As she turned her attention to me, I felt a sudden surge of anxiety, unsure of how to comport myself in the presence of such a powerful and enigmatic figure. Though I knew little of her, my heart swelled with respect and admiration for the Queen, whose reputation for wisdom and strength was known throughout the kingdom.

"And you," she began, her voice soft and measured. "Menoetius' child, you're growing up quite well also. You're starting to resemble your father, but those eyes... those are indeed your mothers."

Despite the Queen's kind words, I felt a twinge of sadness deep within me. While her comment was intended as a compliment, it only served to remind me of the painful truth that I had never known much about my mother, save for the fact that she had died while giving birth to me.

The Queen noticed the sadness etched on my face and spoke in a gentle tone, "Don't be sad, child. You were the pride of Philomela's life. She had yearned for a child with all her heart, and Lady Hera had finally answered her prayers by blessing her with you. Carrying you inside her were the happiest nine months of her entire life."

Her words were like a soothing balm to my wounded heart, and I felt a sense of comfort wash over me. Though I had never known my mother, the Queen's words made me feel as though I had been given a glimpse into her heart, into the love and devotion that she had felt for me even before I had taken my first breath.

"Come dear, sit down. Let's feast!" King Peleus exclaimed, his eyes sparkling with excitement and joy. He beckoned her over with a grand gesture, enfolding her in a warm embrace as he pulled out a chair for her to sit on.

Chapter 3

The sound of music filled the grand hall as the talented musicians played their instruments, their melodies weaving together in perfect harmony. The air was filled with the delicious aroma of food, and the room was alive with laughter and celebration.

Peleus and Achilles were in high spirits, chatting and laughing with Queen Thetis, their faces alight with joy. As I sat there watching, I couldn't help but feel like an outsider, despite their efforts to make me feel included. Even though I wasn't related to them by blood, they had always treated me like family. But in that moment, as they continued to revel in each other's company, I couldn't shake the feeling of being out of place.

My gaze drifted towards Achilles, who had now switched seats and was sitting next to his mother. It had been ages since he had seen her, and I couldn't blame him for wanting to catch up with her. But as he chatted away with the Queen, I couldn't help but feel neglected and forgotten.

Thetis, gazed at her son with a glint of amusement in her eyes. Her lips curled into a playful smile as she asked, "So Achilles, have you found a bride yet?"

Achilles' face flushed with embarrassment at the mention of marriage. "Mother!" he exclaimed.

Thetis leaned back into her chair, her smile growing wider. "Oh, don't 'mother' me," she chided affectionately. "You know that you must find a suitable partner soon. Your father and I met when we were your age, so it's only fitting that you do the same." Her hand reached up to cup his cheek, her touch seemed warm and comforting.

As we approached manhood, Queen Thetis' words resonated with us - it was time to seek out wives. Despite our impending adulthood, the idea of being in a relationship still filled us with a sense of unease and embarrassment.

In a moment of vulnerability, Achilles finally admitted, "Fine...th ere might be one." I was caught off guard by his confession.

Questions flooded my mind. Who was this mysterious girl he spoke of? Why had he not mentioned her before? As his best friend and confidant, I couldn't help but feel a pang of annoyance that he had kept this secret from me.

King Peleus' excitement was palpable as he exclaimed, "It's that Deidamia girl, isn't it!? She's a good girl, I'm certain you'll have some strong and beautiful babies together!"

Achilles let out a groan of embarrassment as his parents chuckled at his discomfort. His face flushed with a mixture of annoyance and bashfulness.

"And what about you, Patroklos? Have you found a girl?" Queen Thetis turned her attention to me and I could feel all eyes in the room on me. But it was Achilles' gaze that felt the most intense, as if he was anticipating for my answer.

"No." I replied with a weak smile, my heart sinking at the thought of disappointing everyone. The truth was, I couldn't possibly find someone when my entire existence revolved around Achilles. How could I possibly have a love life when everything I did was for him? Unless...

But before I could finish my thought, the Queen spoke up again. "Good," she said, her voice firm. "As Achilles' companion, I expect nothing less than your undivided attention."

As Queen Thetis' words sank in, I realized that her question had been a test of my loyalty after all. It seemed that she wanted to see if I took my role as Achilles' companion seriously. And of course, I did. My entire existence was devoted to him and I would do anything to support him.

But as I pondered her motives, I couldn't help but feel a twinge of frustration. Did she not trust me? Did she not trust her own son to choose a companion who would be loyal and dedicated to him?

Despite my inner turmoil, I kept my thoughts to myself and simply nodded in agreement. I knew that my loyalty to Achilles was unwavering, and I hoped that one day Queen Thetis would come to see that as well.

As I lay there in the stillness of the night, the only sounds around us were the soft chirping of crickets and the sound of Achilles' small, steady breaths. But my mind was far from calm as I struggled to contain my anger.

"Why didn't you tell me about Deidamia?" I spoke sternly, trying to keep my emotions in check. I didn't want to show Achilles how angry I was, but it was difficult to hide my frustration.

"What about her?" he asked innocently, his voice calm and soothing. Sometimes I wondered if he was truly clueless or if he was intentionally trying to push my buttons.

My anger boiled over as I spoke, my voice low and menacing. "You know exactly what I mean. Why didn't you tell me that you're interested in Deidamia?"

I heard Achilles shift on his bed, and I turned to face him. In the pale moonlight, his bare chest glimmered, and his bright eyes shone like stars in the dark.

"I'm not interested in Deidamia," he said, his voice calm and steady. "Sure, she's cute, but I have no intention of marrying her."

My anger began to dissipate as Achilles explained himself. "Then why did you lie to your parents?"

"I didn't lie, I just didn't say anything," he chuckled, his voice light and carefree.

I narrowed my eyes at him. "So who is it then?"

Confusion etched across Achilles' face as he struggled to understand my question. "Huh?" he said, his voice laced with confusion.

I repeated myself, my tone insistent. "Who is the person you're interested in? You said you liked someone, so who is it?"

Achilles stared at me intently, his eyes searching mine for something I couldn't quite decipher. The weight of his silence hung heavy in the air, as if he were deliberating whether to reveal a deep, guarded secret. Finally, after what felt like an eternity, he broke the silence.

His voice carried a hint of amusement as he chuckled and remarked, "You're quite nosy, aren't you?"

I couldn't help but feel a surge of frustration at his evasiveness. "Seriously? You're not going to tell me?" I blurted out, unable to contain my curiosity any longer.

"Nope." He said nonchalantly.

My emotions got the better of me, and I found myself blurting out the accusation that had been brewing inside me. "You know you were a jerk today," I spat out, my words laced with resentment. I turned away from him, facing the wall in an attempt to hide my vulnerability.

Achilles's expression remained impassive, but a flicker of surprise crossed his face. "What do you mean?" he exclaimed, genuinely taken aback.

"During training. You were being a dick!" My words hung in the air, charged with the frustration that had been simmering within me. The memory of his behavior during our training session burned in my mind, fueling my outburst

Silence enveloped the room once again, broken only by the sound of Achilles's deep breaths. I could sense him lying back down, his presence still lingering in the room.

Suddenly, his voice pierced through the silence, laced with a hint of amusement. "Not my fault you suck at fighting," he quipped, his laughter echoing softly in the darkness.

Unable to contain my frustration any longer, I grabbed my pillow and hurled it at him in a fit of defiance.

"Ow! Is this how you treat your lord?" he exclaimed, a hint of playfulness in his voice.

"As his chosen companion, it is my duty to guide him," I retorted, sitting back up and meeting his gaze. "Especially when his ego blinds him to his own faults." Though the room was shrouded in darkness, I mustered a small smile, hoping he could sense it.

His response came in the form of a playful threat. "Those are bold words, Patroklos! Be careful, or you might just lose your head."

"If that is your wish, my lord, then so be it," I replied, turning my back to him once again. "I am going to sleep."

Just as I began to settle into the comfort of my bed, I felt a sudden shift in the atmosphere. The sound of his bed sheets rustling reached my ears, and before I could comprehend what was happening, his hand gripped my arm, pulling me to my feet.

"What are you doing?!" I exclaimed, my confusion evident in my voice.

"Fight me," he said calmly, his eyes glinting in the darkness.

Achilles wanted me to engage in a battle, right here in the confines of our room, in the dead of night. He had finally lost his mind.

""You have officially lost your mind," I responded, my voice devoid of any trace of emotion, as if I were merely stating a fact.

Achilles's retort carried a hint of dismissiveness, his words laced with playful taunting. "Oh, shut up and fight me. Come on! Don't be a loser."

The absurdity of his request weighed heavily on my mind. How could he expect me to compete against him when every previous encounter had ended in my defeat? The frustration welled up within me, threatening to spill over. "But I am... every time we fight, I lose," I admitted, my voice tinged with resignation.

Achilles's response, delivered with an air of nonchalance, only fueled my frustration. "Well then... maybe DON'T lose!" His words hung in the air, a simplistic solution that offered no real guidance or strategy.

A heavy sigh escaped my lips, carrying with it a mixture of resignation and weariness. I braced myself for what felt like an inevitable outcome, my muscles tensing in preparation for the impending clash. With a lackluster effort, I threw the first punch, its trajectory lacking the precision and determination it needed. To my surprise, Achilles reacted with a seriousness that belied the dimly lit room, parrying my half-hearted strike with a deftness that sent me stumbling backward, crashing onto his bed.

"Again," he commanded, his voice carrying an unwavering determination, his body already poised to repeat the cycle of this relentless contest.

The fatigue that coursed through my veins seeped into my voice as I mustered a plea, tinged with exhaustion. "I'm tired, and it's too dark to see. Can we just do this in the morning?"

Achilles's response was swift and resolute, leaving no room for negotiation. "I said, again!" His words cut through the air, firm and unwavering, refusing to accept anything less than compliance.

Reluctantly, I readied myself once more, summoning a flicker of determination amidst my weariness. This time, my form held a hint of strength, a glimmer of defiance. I struck out towards him, hoping to catch him off guard, but he effortlessly evaded my attack, swiftly pinning me back onto his bed, our bodies locked in a familiar and frustrating pattern.

We repeated this relentless cycle countless times, each iteration fueling a growing frustration within me. Failure gnawed at my resolve, but a flicker of determination burned bright in my core. I yearned to best Achilles, to prove that I was not bound to a perpetual cycle of defeat. But try as I might, his speed eluded me, his movements a blur of agility and precision.

Finally, Achilles called for a pause, his voice carrying a hint of wisdom amidst the chaos. "Stop and think," he advised, his tone cutting through my haze of emotions. "You're letting your anger control you. You need to plan your next moves, anticipate my actions."

His words struck a chord within me, a reminder that victory lay not in blind fury, but in calculated strategy. I knew that no matter how I attacked, he would effortlessly dodge, seize my arm, and pin me to the bed. I had to adapt, to find a way to overcome his relentless grasp.

Summoning every ounce of focus, I struck at him once more, but this time it was not an aimless flail. I anticipated his next move, my mind working in tandem with my body. As he grabbed my arm, I swiftly kicked the back of his thigh, catching him off guard. The surprise caused him to momentarily loosen his grip, granting me a precious moment of freedom. With a surge of determination, I pulled my arm free, charging my other hand for a strike.

But Achilles, ever vigilant, reacted with lightning speed. He charged at me, his movements fueled by instinct and experience. In an instant, he grabbed my entire torso, overpowering me and pinning me back onto the bed. The weight of his body pressed against mine, his long strands of hair brushing against my face, carrying with them the intoxicating scent of ambrosia. The sweet aroma enveloped me, almost tangible in its intensity, teasing my senses with its alluring presence.

As I struggled to catch my breath, the sound of Achilles' laughter echoed above me, filling the room with a vibrant energy. "Good, now we're getting somewhere," he chuckled, his voice carrying a hint of satisfaction.

I struggled to catch my breath, my muscles fatigued and aching. "Have you had enough fun for one night? We can continue this tomorrow," I suggested, my voice laced with exhaustion.

"Fine, fine. We can go to sleep now. But I expect more of this tomorrow!" he declared, his tone firm and unwavering.

"More of what? Sleep deprivation?" I retorted, my snarky remark barely masking my frustration.

"More of you improving your combat," he clarified, his voice carrying a sense of determination.

"It doesn't feel like I improved at all," I admitted, my shoulders slumping in defeat. Despite my best efforts, Achilles had still managed to best me.

"Don't sell yourself short! You almost brought me to my knees," he countered, his hand patting my head in a gesture of reassurance.

"Your knees barely moved an inch," I pointed out, my voice tinged with bitterness.

"Still, barely an inch closer than anyone else has managed to," he replied, his words carrying a sense of pride. With that, he fell back onto the bed, his body relaxing into a state of peaceful slumber.

I clambered off his bed, my body still pulsing with the remnants of our intense sparring session. As I lay down on my own bed, I glanced back at Achilles. His breathing was slow and steady, a cadence of tranquility that seemed to wash away the tensions of the day. In the soft glow of moonlight, he lay there, resembling a slumbering babe, untouched by the worries and burdens of the world.

Chapter 4

Achilles and I had spent countless hours training with the most renowned warriors in all of Greece, but none of them compared to the legendary Lord Chiron, whom we were about to meet today.

Lord Chiron had struck a deal with King Peleus, allowing Achilles and me the privilege of being trained under his tutelage. It was an opportunity like no other, a chance to learn skills and techniques that no other warrior had ever mastered.

Achilles was positively ecstatic, his excitement practically radiating off him. "I can't believe it! We're actually going to be trained by Lord Chiron himself!" he exclaimed, unable to contain his joy. I couldn't help but smile at his enthusiasm, though I had lost count of how many times he had repeated that same sentence throughout the day.

As we waited for our meeting with Lord Chiron, I suggested that we engage in other activities to pass the time. Perhaps we could read, practice playing the lyre, or even play a game. However,

Achilles was far too preoccupied with his anticipation and couldn't focus on anything else.

Finally, unable to bear his incessant pacing any longer, I grabbed Achilles by the arm and spoke out of frustration. It was a rare moment of assertiveness from me, as I had never demanded anything from him before. But the constant pacing was becoming unbearable, and I had reached my limit.

Achilles was taken aback by my sudden change in demeanor. He had never heard me order him to do anything before, and it was certainly not how our interactions were supposed to go. But I had grown tired of his restlessness and felt compelled to speak up.

"Pacing around aimlessly isn't going to accomplish anything," I said firmly, trying to keep my frustration in check. "I understand that you're excited, but we shouldn't waste our time like this. Can we please do something productive before we leave? We have no idea when we'll be back."

Achilles seemed to snap out of his shocked state and nodded in agreement. "You're right. It's foolish to waste our precious time doing nothing," he admitted. With a playful glint in his oceanic eyes, he grabbed my hand and led the way. "Come, let's visit the Agora."

Normally, we would visit the bustling marketplace twice a month, always accompanied by guards. However, this time we ventured out on our own, feeling a newfound sense of freedom.

Along the way, Achilles managed to procure two cloaks from a random house, which we used to conceal our identities. As we entered the Agora, a vibrant and bustling scene greeted us. People meandered through the crowded markets, their arms laden with various goods - food, drinks, jewelry, clothing, and even weapons and armor.

The bright colors of blue and white adorned the attire of the locals, providing some respite from the scorching sun. Men wore tunics that fell just above their thighs, while women's garments flowed all the way down to their feet.

We strolled through the winding streets, taking in the sights and sounds of the marketplace. Achilles, always the playful one, picked up a flowing red dress meant for women and jokingly draped it over himself. "So, how do I look?" he quipped, a mischievous grin lighting up his face.

"If it were a competition, Helen would surely pale in comparison," I replied, referring to Helen of Sparta, renowned as the most beautiful woman in all of Greece. We had caught a glimpse of her at her wedding to King Menelaus, and her ethereal beauty was truly unmatched.

It was quite uncommon for women to marry at the age of nineteen, as it was considered relatively older. However, Helen's extraordinary beauty made her an irresistible prospect for any man.

Her husband, Menelaus, the powerful king of Sparta, reigned over one of the strongest nations in the Greek world and it was widely known that he and Helen were deeply and passionately in love.

As we continued our exploration of the Agora, my attention was drawn to a small stall displaying a pair of intricately crafted dice. I couldn't explain why, but I felt an inexplicable desire to own them. As I ran my fingers over the smooth oak wood, I was reminded of my late father, with whom I had played dice before his passing. The dice before me seemed to hold a sentimental value, so without hesitation, I purchased them.

With the dice in hand, we decided it was time to head back home. As we left the lively marketplace behind, I couldn't help but feel a sense of contentment. Our visit to the Agora had been a welcome respite from our usual rigorous training, and the small trinket I had acquired served as a cherished reminder of my father's memory.

As we retraced our steps through the bustling streets, a sudden interruption halted our progress. A young man, with a twitching hand and a cloak that barely concealed his unkempt appearance, approached us in a whirlwind of rapid speech.

"Hey! Wannaseemywares? I havethegreatest stuff inthe entire Agora! Come takea look!" His words tumbled out in a jumbled rush, barely comprehensible amidst the speed of his delivery.

Taken aback by his sudden appearance, I couldn't help but notice the filth that clung to him, emanating a pungent stench. Despite my reservations, Achilles, ever curious, approached the man.

"What are you selling?" Achilles inquired, his voice laced with a hint of caution.

"Only the finest things," the man replied, beckoning us to follow him down a dimly lit alleyway. Though I felt a twinge of unease, I followed closely beside Achilles, my hand instinctively reaching for the concealed spear sheathed beneath my cloak.

As we ventured further into the alley, my apprehension grew, and my senses sharpened. I had expected the man's promised wares to materialize, but instead, we were met with the sudden appearance of two other shadowy figures, their knives glinting ominously in the dim light.

"Give us everything you have!" One of them bellowed from behind, his voice dripping with menace.

Whispering urgently to Achilles, I voiced my concern. "Achilles, what do we do?" I asked, my voice laden with anxiety.

Though we had been trained to face formidable foes on the battlefield, and these were just common criminals, I couldn't help but fear for our lives. This was no mere training exercise; it was a perilous encounter with real danger.

In that moment, Achilles erupted into laughter, a sound that reverberated through the narrow alley. I couldn't discern whether I should be more frightened of him or the criminals themselves.

"Do you really think you can rob us? Do you have any idea who I am?" Achilles declared, his laughter tinged with anger and pride as he shed his cloak. "I am Prince Achilles, son of King Peleus, ruler of this very land upon which you pathetic lowlifes tread!" His voice thundered with authority and indignation.

"Shit! It's actually the Prince! We should get out of here quickly, before the guards come!" One of the criminals with a red cloth covering his face exclaimed, panic creeping into his voice.

"No," the other criminal retorted swiftly. "They have cloaks on. No one knows they're here except us. We can take them and have them ransomed by the King. We'd make so much more money this way." A sinister smile played upon his lips as he continued to mumble his words, revealing his decayed teeth.

"If you dare to attack us, the only payment you'll receive is with your own blood," Achilles warned, his hand poised on the hilt of his sheathed spear.

"Isn't the little Prince just adorable with his brave words," the man sneered, his gaze shifting towards me. "Whataboutyou? Cat got your tongue?" A sense of dread washed over me, stronger than before. I could see the malice in his eyes, realizing that he now only needed Achilles alive, while I was merely a "fun" bonus.

Achilles swiftly positioned himself in front of me, shielding me from the man's gaze.

"Isn't this cute? Attack them!" the criminal commanded. In an instant, the two men behind us lunged forward, their movements fueled by aggression and desperation.

"Back-Turn!" Achilles commanded. Reacting instinctively, I spun around, pressing my back against his, effectively swapping positions. In that moment, my training took over, guiding my actions as Achilles employed his well-practiced commands.

Now facing the man who had led us into this treacherous situation, I unsheathed my spear, extending it to its full length with a deft press of a button beneath my thumb.

As Achilles battled the men behind me, their clash of weapons reverberated through the air, a symphony of danger and adrenaline. Though I couldn't witness the precise details of their confrontation, I could discern the unmistakable sound of Achilles' thick spear slicing through the air with lethal precision.

Fear coursed through my veins, threatening to paralyze me, but I knew there was no time for hesitation. I had to fight for my life. The man before me brandished a gleaming knife, a weapon that required close proximity to be effective. I understood that as long as I kept him at a distance, I could maintain control of the situation.

Gripping my spear tightly, I pointed its sharp tip towards him, my muscles tense and ready to strike. The defensive stance I adopted seemed to aggravate him, evident from the frustration etched upon his face.

"Getoverhere already!" he bellowed, charging towards me with a ferocity that belied his grimy appearance. Despite my efforts to keep him at bay, he managed to evade my spear and forcefully pushed me to the ground.

The impact sent a jolt of pain through my body as my head and back collided with the dirty floor. For a brief moment, my vision blurred, disorienting me. As it gradually cleared, I found myself pinned beneath the weight of the man, his hands closing around my throat with a vice-like grip.

Breathing became a struggle, panic gripping me tightly. I thrashed my arms desperately, but my feeble attempts proved futile against his superior strength. Even without his hands around my throat, I felt powerless and vulnerable. Without my spear, I was rendered defenseless, my training useless.

My limbs grew heavy, my vision dimming as the lack of oxygen took its toll. I lay there, helpless and resigned to my fate. This was the end...

In that moment of despair, a single word echoed in my mind, a lifeline in the darkness. "Achilles..."

Summoning the last vestiges of my strength, I uttered his name aloud. And in a heartbeat, the man's expression transformed from a wicked grin to a mask of shock and pain.

I watched, breathless, as Achilles' golden spear pierced through the man's open mouth, silencing him forever. The tension on my neck released, and I gasped for air, coughing violently as my body fought to recover.

As my vision cleared, I surveyed the aftermath of Achilles' lethal prowess. The lifeless bodies of our assailants lay strewn across the ground, testaments to his skill and ruthlessness. And yet, as I looked at Achilles, a grin of enjoyment etched upon his face, a chill ran down my spine. He reveled in this violence, this dance of death.

Attempting to rise, I felt a sharp pain in my side. Blood stained my clothes, a mix of my own and that of the fallen thug. Confusion clouded my thoughts as I stared at the knife lodged within me, its presence surreal and disorienting. I didn't know what to do, my mind blank with shock and disbelief.

"You're hurt!" Achilles exclaimed, concern etching his features as he crouched beside me. "What should I do?" he asked urgently.

Confusion knitted my brow as I gazed at Achilles, my mind a swirling tempest of uncertainty. "I don't know," I admitted, my voice tinged with frustration and a tinge of disappointment in myself.

His eyes widened with concern, his brows furrowing as he contemplated the situation. "Should I pull it out?" he asked, his voice laced with urgency.

Once again, I found myself at a loss, my mind unable to grasp a solution. "I don't know," I repeated, my voice barely above a whisper.

I had always relied on Achilles to have all the answers, to know better. After all, he was the Prince, the embodiment of strength and wisdom. But in that moment, I realized that I too should possess some semblance of capability.

Frustration welled within me, threatening to consume my thoughts, but before I could dwell further on my own perceived incompetence, a heavy weariness washed over me. Fatigue settled into my bones, my body succumbing to the weight of the situation.

My vision, already blurred by the pain and chaos, began to fade, like a flickering candle slowly extinguishing. Achilles' voice echoed in the distance, a mere whisper against the encroaching darkness. And then, as if swallowed by an abyss, everything plunged into an inky blackness.

Chapter 5

As I slowly regained consciousness, the gentle symphony of crickets filled the air, their melodious chirping acting as a soothing lullaby. My eyes fluttered open, and as I took in my surroundings, I found myself in the infirmary. The room exuded a sense of calm, with its sterile white walls and neatly arranged medical equipment.

As my gaze wandered, I couldn't help but be captivated by the scene outside the window. The night sky stretched out before me, its vast expanse painted in a velvety black hue. Countless stars adorned the celestial canvas, twinkling like tiny diamonds, illuminating the darkness with their ethereal glow.

Suddenly, a familiar voice resonated beside me, causing me to startle. It was King Peleus, standing by my bedside. The unexpected presence of another person in the room initially jolted me, but as I recognized the regal figure before me, a sense of relief washed over me. His warm and caring demeanor immediately put me at ease.

"Patroklos," he spoke with a tender tone, his voice carrying the weight of a concerned father. "How are you feeling, my son?"

"I'm-" A sharp pang of agony shot through my body as I attempted to rise from the softness of my pillow. Gritting my teeth, I fought against the searing pain that radiated from my side.

"Don't move, Patroklos! You might reopen your wound." King Peleus warned me with concern.

In that moment, a sinking feeling overwhelmed me as I realized that he was the sole presence in the room. My gaze darted around, desperately searching for Achilles, but he was nowhere to be found.

Before I could even voice my question, the King interrupted me abruptly, as if he had anticipated my inquiry. "He's left. Lord Chiron took him away an hour ago."

The words struck me like a blow, and I struggled to form a coherent sentence amidst the chaos of my racing thoughts. "What... No... I must..." My words faltered, unable to convey the urgency and desperation that coursed through me. "I... I must..."

"You must sit and allow yourself to heal," the King's voice commanded with a firm tone. "Your injury is severe, and it is simply not feasible for you to embark on a journey in your current state, Patroklos."

"But I am his loyal companion! I am meant to be by his side, no matter the circumstances!"

Acknowledging my loyalty, the King's expression softened. "Indeed, you are his steadfast companion," he affirmed. "However, it was Achilles himself who ordered that you remain here and focus on your recovery. If you truly wish to honor your bond, you must heed his wishes. Now, rest. I shall instruct the servants to bring you food."

Although I understood that King Peleus was genuinely concerned for my well-being and felt obliged to ensure I followed Achilles' orders, I knew deep down that I could not simply remain idle and confined within the walls of the palace.

With a determined resolve, I pushed the sheets off me and swung my legs over the side of the bed. The sharp pain that shot through my body caused me to gasp, and I struggled to control my breathing.

Grimacing, I reached for my spear, which lay on the nearby table, and unsheathed it, using it as a makeshift crutch to support my weight as I hobbled towards the door.

Despite the agony that wracked my body, I managed to dress myself hastily, albeit sloppily, and made my way towards the stables, my mind set on finding a way to reach Achilles.

With great effort, I climbed onto my trusty mare, her white coat shining in the moonlight. The simple act of mounting her was a feat in itself, and I winced as my injured side protested at the movement. But I gritted my teeth and urged her forward, my eyes fixed on the distant mountains.

As I galloped towards our destination, I couldn't help but feel a sense of unease. Lord Chiron's whereabouts were shrouded in mystery, and despite King Peleus' friendship with him, even he didn't know where he lived. The King had a way to communicate with him if necessary, but that was the extent of his knowledge.

The suffocating darkness of the night enveloped me as I pressed forward, my wounded body aching with every step. The dense canopy of trees overhead blocked out any trace of moonlight, leaving me to navigate blindly through the terrain.

With each jarring gallop of my horse, a searing pain shot through my side, intensifying with every beat of my heart. The warm stickiness that coated my trembling fingers confirmed my fears - blood.

My wound had reopened, and I was losing precious life-force with every passing moment.

A sudden crackling noise erupted from behind me, shattering the already tense silence of the forest. Startled, my horse bolted forward, its hooves pounding against the forest floor, desperately trying to outrun the unseen threat.

I clung to the reins with a white-knuckled grip, my heart pounding in my chest, but the wild ride proved too much. In the frenzy, my head collided with a low-hanging tree branch, the impact sending a jolt of pain through my skull. With a sickening thud, I was violently thrown from the mare, my body crashing onto the unforgiving ground.

Agonizing cries tore from my lips as the open wound on my side throbbed with excruciating intensity. The world around me spun, my head swimming with dizziness, while a nauseating sensation churned in the pit of my stomach, threatening to unleash its contents.

Then, amidst the chaos, the crackling of twigs resumed, drawing closer with each passing second before abruptly ceasing. The abrupt silence sent a shiver down my spine, and a paralyzing fear gripped me like never before. The terror of facing this unknown danger in the dark depths of the forest surpassed even the earlier battle against the thugs that had left me wounded.

Summoning every ounce of strength, I forced myself to rise, desperately attempting to flee from the encroaching danger. But my body betrayed me only a few seconds later, giving way beneath the weight of my injuries. I crumpled to the ground, the world around me fading into an abyss of darkness as consciousness slipped away.

As the scent of savory food wafted through the air, mingling with the comforting crackle of the fire, my senses snapped to attention. The sound of the wood popping and hissing sent a jolt of adrenaline coursing through my veins, bringing me to full alertness in an instant.

Grimacing in pain, I clutched my injured side, determined to push through the agony. Slowly, I surveyed my surroundings, my eyes widening as they landed on a figure seated by the flickering flames.

"Who-Who are you?!" I bellowed, my voice trembling with a mix of fear and feeble attempts at intimidation. Deep down, I knew that my words held little power, and I couldn't help but feel like a frightened child in the face of the unknown.

The man, now risen from his seated position, approached the bubbling pot with purpose. His eyes, fixed on me, held a mix of curiosity and something else I couldn't quite decipher. As he stirred the pot slowly, his movements deliberate and controlled, his voice cutting through the silence.

"The man who saved your life," he declared, his words hanging in the air. The weight of his statement hit me like a sudden gust of wind, causing my heart to skip a beat. I couldn't help but wonder how close I had come to meeting, Thanatos.

His gaze remained fixed on me, as if trying to unravel some hidden truth. "I guess your parents never taught you manners?" he mused, his tone tinged with a hint of reproach. "People usually say 'thank you' after someone saves their life."

A mixture of embarrassment and gratitude washed over me, and I stumbled to find the right words to express my appreciation. But before I could respond, my attention was drawn to the cave's contents. Spears, swords, and shields adorned one corner, their gleaming surfaces catching the flickering light. Across from them, a simple bed beckoned, offering a semblance of comfort in this rugged environment.

Returning my gaze to the man, I couldn't help but feel a sense of familiarity. His features were etched with lines of experience, his eyes holding a glimmer of wisdom. Could this be...?

"Most people also believe that staring is considered rude," he commented, breaking the silence. His words snapped me out of my thoughts, and I realized that I had been scrutinizing him intently, searching for answers in his face.

Caught off guard, I stammered, "You... have been staring at me the whole time as well."

A mischievous glint danced in his eyes as he continued to fix his gaze upon me, intensifying my discomfort. The weight of his scrutiny seemed to penetrate my very core, making me squirm under its intensity.

"Well, I'm not most people," he chuckled, breaking the tension. With a practiced hand, he ladled a generous portion of stew into a bowl, the fragrant steam rising in wisps. "Here, eat."

He approached me and although I flinched backwards he still proceeded on giving me the food.

"When you're finished, come find me outside," he instructed, his voice filled with an air of mystery. With those words, he turned and left, leaving me alone in the dimly lit cave, my thoughts swirling like the shadows dancing on the walls.

One glance at the steaming stew was all it took for my stomach to growl in anticipation. The hunger pangs intensified, reminding me that I hadn't eaten anything since the morning prior. With a mix of trepidation and need, I began gobbling down the food, the warmth and nourishment flooding my senses. A sharp pain shot through my stomach, a reminder of its emptiness and my body's weakened state.

As I savored the last spoonful of stew, a wave of longing washed over me, begging for more. The flavors lingered on my tongue, tempting me to indulge further. However, a sense of restraint prevailed within me. The man before me, whom I desperately hoped was Lord Chiron, had not only saved my life but also provided nourishment when I needed it most. I couldn't risk angering him or appearing ungrateful for his benevolence.

Emerging from the dimly lit cave, I was momentarily blinded by the intensity of the sun's rays. Shielding my eyes with a hand, I surveyed my surroundings, hoping to catch sight of the enigmatic man who had saved me. But all I could see was an endless expanse of towering trees, their branches reaching towards the heavens like silent sentinels.

Confusion gnawed at my mind as I tried to make sense of the smaller red trees mixed among the green ones. I was certain those were ambrosia trees, indicating that I was still in Myrmidon. The city I called home was the only place on this world that could grow ambrosia trees but never had I seen so many in one place. Our land was the sole fertile place capable of nurturing these trees, and even then, it was an arduous task to cultivate just one. Fortunately, through immense effort and unwavering dedication, we had succeeded in growing numerous ambrosia trees, and we thrived as a result.

Just as my thoughts began to spiral, a voice broke through the silence, causing me to startle. "There you are," The man had appeared behind me, his presence both reassuring and mysterious. In his outstretched hand, he held my silver spear, its surface gleaming in the sunlight. I reached out to take it, feeling the familiar weight in my grasp. "You forgot this."

Using the spear as a makeshift support, I steadied myself, mindful of the wound that still throbbed with pain. Though the ache had dulled since the man's healing touch, I knew better than to push my limits. The events of the previous day still lingered in my memory, a reminder of my vulnerability and the need for caution.

Seeking answers, I turned to the enigmatic man and posed the question that burned within me. "Where are we?" I inquired, my voice laced with a mixture of curiosity and apprehension.

His response came without hesitation, yet it offered little solace. "The forest," he replied, his tone devoid of emotion.

Frustration welled within me as I pressed for further clarification. "I know that, but... where exactly?" I implored, hoping to elicit a more specific response.

"A mountain, in the forest," he replied once again, his words dripping with a dryness that matched his unyielding demeanor.

I let out a sigh, realizing that he wasn't going to divulge any further details. "You're not going to tell me, are you?" I asked, my voice tinged with exasperation.

"No," he said simply, his gaze meeting mine with an intensity that made me uneasy.

His voice took on a more serious tone as he continued, revealing a glimpse of the purpose behind my presence. "I was asked to train the sons of Peleus, but only one was ready. The other was not. Yet, despite your condition-half-dead and bearing a foolish bruise on your head-you still showed up."

My fingers instinctively grazed the tender spot on my head, a reminder of the sharp impact from the wayward tree branch that had struck me.

"So tell me then boy. Who are you?" He inquired, his voice carrying a weight of authority and intrigue.

"Patro-" I began, but before I could utter my full name, a sharp smack landed on the back of my head, causing me to wince in pain. Confusion and irritation mingled within me as I instinctively rubbed the affected area. "Ow! What was that for?" I protested, my voice laced with a mixture of surprise and indignation.

His gaze remained unyielding, undeterred by my reaction. "I already know your name," he retorted, his tone firm. "I'm asking, who are you?"

My mind raced as I grappled with the weighty question, attempting to find the words that would satisfy his inquiry. However, before I could formulate a response, the sting of another blow landed forcefully on the back of my head, jolting me from my thoughts.

The man's voice took on a more menacing tone, laced with a hint of impatience. "Who are you, boy? What brings you to this place?" His words reverberated through the air, carrying an undertone of threat that sent a shiver down my spine.

Stumbling slightly, I instinctively took a step back, my eyes locked on his imposing figure. The fear within me mingled with a growing sense of defiance. "I... I am Achilles' chosen companion," I managed to utter, my voice quivering with a mixture of determination and uncertainty.

Attempting to create distance between us, I cautiously continued to retreat. However, to my dismay, I underestimated the man's reach. From under his arm, he revealed a slender stick, hidden until now, and with swift precision, he struck me once again, this time from a distance. The sharp impact reverberated through my head.

"Great title, but I didn't ask for it. Why are you here boy?" The man's voice remained steady, yet an unsettling shift occurred in his presence, intensifying the air of menace that surrounded him.

Struggling to find my voice amidst the growing unease, I stammered, "I... I am bound to be at his side, no matter the circumstances." The conviction in my words wavered, overshadowed by the uncertainty that lingered within me.

Without striking me this time, he continued his probing. "So, it is loyalty that drives you? Or perhaps it is a lack of purpose in your own life, leading you to seek solace in living beneath another man's shadow?"

I tried to respond, to defend my choices, but my words dissolved into thin air as another blow landed upon me. Though the strikes did not inflict any physical harm, they stung, disrupting my train of thought with each impact. Frustration welled within me as I struggled to maintain focus, the blows becoming a relentless hindrance to my ability to articulate my thoughts.

Each strike landed with a resounding thud, the force of each blow reverberating through my body, jolting me with a mix of pain and frustration. The relentless assault had taken its toll, pushing me to the brink of endurance.

But then, something within me snapped. The pent-up anger and confusion surged forth, fueling my voice as I unleashed a primal scream. "I DON'T KNOW!" I bellowed, my words echoing in the air, a raw expression of my inner turmoil. The grip on my spear tightened to the point of pain, my knuckles turning white as I clung to the weapon for support.

In a surge of adrenaline-fueled anger, I swung my spear towards him, immediately regretting it. In an instant, a vicious strike met my face, sending me sprawling backward, my body crashing onto the unforgiving ground.

As I lay there, dazed and disoriented, my vision blurred, and the world around me faded into a blinding white. Time seemed to stand still, each passing moment stretching into an eternity as I struggled to regain my senses.

A mocking laughter pierced through the haze, cutting through the silence. "Well, well," he taunted, his voice laced with a mix of surprise and amusement. "There is fire in you after all." His words hung in the air, a testament to the unexpected strength I had displayed. "Who would have thought? Not even Achilles had the guts to attack me when I subjected him to the same treatment."

Confusion etched itself into every line of my face as I regarded him with a puzzled expression. "What was the point of that?" I asked, my voice laced with a mix of curiosity and frustration.

"To see if you're worth being taught what I'm going to teach you," he replied, his tone matter-of-fact. "Achilles was just like everyone else in this world. Strong, ambitious, and full of youthful ego. But you... you're different."

I shook my head, my scepticism growing by the second. "You don't know anything about me. You just met me."

"But I do," he countered, his voice low and steady. "You just don't know you yet. Right now, you follow your Lord blindly. You act like you have a purpose to serve him, but deep inside, there's something else. Your true purpose for existing, and I will help you realise it."

He extended his arm, offering me a hand, and pulled me back up to my feet. "You'll call me Lord Chiron from now on, and you will obey my orders. Is that clear, boy?"

I regarded him with a strange mix of apprehension and curiosity, unsure of what to make of this enigmatic figure who had suddenly appeared in my life. He didn't fit the meld of what I had imagined him to be, based on all the stories I had heard of him. But perhaps that was the mark of a true legend - someone who was unafraid to think outside the box and challenge convention.

Despite my reservations, I found myself inexplicably drawn to him, a sense of trust growing within me. He saw something in me that no one else had, and for that, I was willing to follow him wherever he led me.

"Yes, sir," I replied, my voice barely above a whisper, but brimming with unwavering resolve.

Chapter 6

It had been a long and transformative journey of two yearss since I first embarked on my training under the wise and revered Lord Chiron. The passage of time had not only honed my skills but also enriched my mind with a vast array of knowledge that was highly sought after by many. The privilege of receiving such teachings was not lost on me.

As I stood in the midst of a serene landscape, Lord Chiron's voice, filled with patience and wisdom, resonated softly in my ears. His guidance was a constant reminder of the immense responsibility that came with my training.

With focused determination, I carefully positioned my self-crafted bow, its intricate details a testament to the countless hours I had spent perfecting my craft. Ahead of me, a graceful deer grazed peacefully in a meadow, blissfully unaware of our presence.

Both Achilles and I had been fortunate enough to witness the masterful hunts of Lord Chiron. Under his expert guidance, we had learned the art of crafting our own bows and arrows, honing our skills in archery, and mastering the delicate art of tracking down our prey. But Lord Chiron's teachings went beyond the mere mechanics of hunting; he instilled in us a deep reverence for the creatures we would inevitably take the lives of, reminding us to honor their sacrifice so that we could sustain our own.

As we stood in the presence of the majestic Lord Chiron, his voice resonated with a blend of authority and compassion. His words carried the weight of countless years of wisdom. "Remember," he began, his voice laced with instruction, "breathe in and let your focus lock onto your target. When you are ready, exhale and release the arrow, allowing your skill and intention to merge in perfect harmony."

I drew in a deep breath, feeling my heart rate slow as I steadied my aim on the unsuspecting deer. With a practiced hand, I released the arrow, watching as it soared through the air and struck the animal with a resounding thud. For a moment, I thought I had missed my target, but then I heard the deer's mournful moan, and I realized that I had indeed hit it. A surge of pride and excitement coursed through me. 'I hit it!' I thought to myself, feeling a sense of accomplishment wash over me.

"Bravo, Patroklos." Lord Chiron's approving voice broke through my reverie, and I turned to him, feeling a sense of validation at his praise.

"Finally, I'm starving." Achilles let out a chuckle from beside me. His hunting skills were already well-established, and he had taken down his fair share of prey. He was a true natural with the bow, as well as with the lyre and spear.

I couldn't help but roll my eyes at his comment, a smirk playing at the corners of my lips. "If you're that hungry, you could have always gone hunting on your own," I quipped, the sarcasm dripping from my words.

Achilles shot me a playful grin, his eyes sparkling with amusement. "I could have but I didn't want to steal your moment." He retorted, his tone light-hearted.

"Enough." Lord Chiron's voice cut through our banter, reminding us of the task at hand. "The deer is still alive, Patroklos. You know what you must do." The deer still lay wounded, its fate resting in my hands. His words were gentle yet firm, a reminder of the solemn responsibility that came with taking the life of another creature.

With guidance from Lord Chiron, Achilles had been gradually discovering the various capabilities of his unique spear. He now skillfully unsheathed it, allowing only the blade to emerge from the top.

As Achilles entrusted the weapon to my trembling hands, I clutched it tightly, feeling its weight and coldness seep into my very being. Desperation flooded my thoughts, for I had prayed fervently that this moment would never come to pass. Yet, against all hopes, it had become a harsh reality. My arrow had missed its mark, and now the poor creature lay before me, its anguished groans piercing the air, a haunting testament to my failure.

"The longer you hesitate, the more the animal suffers," Lord Chiron's voice resonated with a mix of compassion and urgency, his words a somber reminder of the dire situation.

My breaths quivered, each inhalation a struggle to steady my racing heart. My hands trembled uncontrollably, betraying the turmoil that raged within me. Summoning every ounce of willpower, I drew in a deep breath, attempting to regain composure. But the weight of the moment proved overwhelming, and my attempts at self-control proved futile, as my inner turmoil threatened to consume me whole.

I couldn't bear to remain idle any longer, watching the creature writhing in agony. A surge of determination coursed through me, urging me to take action. With a resolute breath, I mustered the strength to drive the weapon towards what I believed to be its heart. The blade pierced the air with a swift, decisive motion. My entire being recoiled, my eyes instinctively squeezing shut, unable to witness the outcome.

Silence settled upon the scene, broken only by the echo of my pounding heart. Slowly, cautiously, I dared to open my eyes, bracing myself for the sight that awaited me. There, before me, lay the deer, its once vibrant form now still and lifeless. A pang of remorse gripped my soul, and I found myself whispering an apology so faint, it was barely audible even to my own ears.

"I'm sorry," I murmured, the words a fragile offering to the fallen creature, as if seeking solace in the midst of my own conflicted emotions.

"You did well, Patroklos. I'll carry it back home, and you will prepare it." Lord Chiron announced as he lifted the body onto his shoulders, his long dark brown hair becoming soaked in blood, as did his exposed back.

Achilles extended his hand towards me, his fingers outstretched in a gesture of assistance. I let out a deep sigh before grasping his hand, using his strength to pull myself up from the ground.

Achilles flashed a cocky smile as he spoke, his words dripping with a playful tone. "I only wanted my spear back, but I guess pulling yourself up works too. You're welcome." He said, relishing in his own wit.

My expression remained neutral as I regarded him, unimpressed by his attempt at humor.

"Fuck you." I muttered under my breath as I turned to walk away.

Achilles quickly realized his mistake and jogged to catch up to me. "Hey, I was joking! Come on, I'm just trying to cheer you up." He said, positioning himself in front of me to block my path. "It was just a joke, I promise."

"It's not about that," I replied, my voice heavy with emotion. The memory of the deer was weighing heavily on my heart.

"Then what is it?" he asked, his concern evident in his expression.

"The deer...the way it looked at me, it was sad," I explained, my voice barely above a whisper. The image of the deer's mournful eyes was replaying inside my mind.

"Well, it was dying. How else would it look?" Achilles retorted, his voice laced with a hint of indifference.

I let out a frustrated yell, unable to contain my exasperation any longer. "Are you seriously this clueless, Achilles?! Do you not feel a shred of sadness when you take a life? When you extinguish someone else's existence?"

"Why would I?" Achilles replied, his tone nonchalant as he shrugged lazily. "Death is an inevitable part of life. You live, and then you die. It's as simple as that." He seemed unfazed by the weight of his words. "That's why you have to become a legend! So that no one ever forgets your name, and therefore you'll live for eternity!"

"You don't have to be a merciless killer to be remembered!" I shouted, my voice filled with desperation. I hoped that my words would penetrate his stubborn facade. "Is that truly what you want your legacy to be? A trail of blood left behind in the pursuit of glory?" I implored, hoping to make him understand. "When you killed those thugs in that alley, you were laughing. You revelled in it. But did you even take a single moment to look into their eyes and witness the life fading away? I have never seen something so horrific..." The memory of their lifeless eyes haunted me, etching a deep sadness within my soul.

Achilles' expression underwent a chilling transformation as soon as I finished speaking. The warmth in his eyes vanished, replaced by an icy detachment that sent shivers down my spine.

"I did," he responded, his voice devoid of its usual playfulness. "I did look at them, and I enjoyed it. I relished in their deaths, but it wasn't for the sheer pleasure of it. Otherwise, you would see me slaughtering people indiscriminately, without reason. I killed those thugs because they posed a threat to your life. I don't care how sorrowful their eyes may have been, or how much I should be burdened with shame for finding pleasure in it. I did it for the right reasons." He turned abruptly, his back now facing me. The tension in his stance was palpable. "Just because death doesn't affect me in the same way it affects you, it doesn't mean I am heartless."

Achilles marched away.

After reluctantly leaving the scene of the deer, I made my way back to my humble abode, a small cave where I had first encountered Lord Chiron. With his guidance, I began the arduous task of preparing the deer, its blood staining my hands and clothes, leaving a distinct, rusty scent in the air.

Lord Chiron, ever watchful, oversaw my efforts, offering advice and guidance as I worked. By the time I had finished, I was covered in a dry, dark residue of blood, a stark reminder of the life that had been taken.

Sensing my weariness, Lord Chiron gently instructed me to cleanse myself in one of the nearby rivers. Not the one we relied on for drinking, of course. With a mix of exhaustion and anticipation, I followed his guidance, finding solace in the thought of washing away the physical and emotional weight that clung to me.

As I reached the riverbank, I shed my clothes, leaving behind the remnants of the hunt. The chilly water greeted me, causing an immediate reaction in my body as goosebumps formed and a shiver ran down my spine. I hesitated for a moment, bracing myself for the cold embrace, before stepping into the river, the water rising from my ankles all the way up to my hips.

"Hey," a familiar voice broke the silence, and I turned to see Achilles approaching, his presence both comforting and unexpected.

"Hey," I managed a weak smile, grateful for him coming here.

"Can I join?" Achilles asked, his voice carrying a hint of vulnerability.

"Sure," I replied, a mix of surprise and relief washing over me.

Achilles slowly began removing his tunic, and though I averted my gaze out of respect, the familiarity of our shared history allowed for a certain level of comfort in this moment.

As he stepped into the river, the water proved deeper than expected, submerging his lower body up to his hips. The shock of the frigid temperature jolted through him, causing a high-pitched scream to escape his lips-a sound I had never heard from him before, nor did I ever anticipate hearing.

"OH MY GODS! IT'S FREEZING COLD!!" Achilles shrieked, his voice filled with a mixture of surprise and disbelief.

Unable to contain myself, I burst into laughter, the sound echoing through the serene surroundings.

"Stop laughing! It isn't funny!" Achilles retorted, annoyance lacing his words.

"But it's quite funny," I managed to respond between chuckles, finding amusement in the unexpected reaction.

For a moment, we locked eyes, our laughter fading, replaced by a shared understanding and a sense of camaraderie. And then, as if unable to resist the infectious joy, we both erupted into laughter once more.

After a while of simply floating in the river, finding solace in its gentle embrace, I mustered the courage to break the silence.

"I'm sorry for what I said earlier. I realize now that your love for fighting doesn't make you a bad person. I shouldn't have insinuated otherwise," I spoke, my voice carrying a mix of sincerity and remorse.

Achilles met my gaze, his eyes filled with understanding and compassion. "I'm sorry too, I know you were upset and saying those things wasn't right. I know how badly the death of your father has upset you." He responded softly, his voice like a delicate feather drifting across a vast ocean.

I sighed, the weight of my emotions palpable. "You're right about my father. His death has left an indelible scar on my heart, a wound that will never fully heal no matter how much I try. I just hate seeing people losing their lives for nothing. Those thugs were bad men but maybe they weren't always like that. Maybe they were driven by desperation, by the need to provide for their families or escape a life of hardship....or maybe they were actually just horrible people, but we can't just kill them."

"They were going to kill us. What else would you have had me do?" Achilles questioned, his voice tinged with a hint of frustration.

"You're right, and I am grateful for saving me. But there's always another way. We could have incapacitated them, handed them over to the authorities. They could have faced justice, had a chance to atone and perhaps even change."

"Or they could have been released, only to continue robbing and killing." He countered.

"Perhaps," I conceded, my voice laced with uncertainty. "But it's their right to try. We can't deny them that opportunity."

We continued to float side by side, our elbows occasionally brushing against each other. In the quietude of the moment, Achilles spoke my name, his voice filled with a tenderness that sent a gentle ripple through my heart.

"Patroklos..."

"Yes?" I responded, my voice barely a whisper.

"You have a heart that cares deeply. I've never met anyone quite like you. Your ability to see the good in others, even when they don't deserve it... it's a beautiful thing. I'm grateful to have you by my side," he confessed, his words enveloping me like a warm embrace.

His admission caused my heart to skip a beat, a rush of warmth flooding through me. "And I too am grateful to stand beside you," I replied, my voice filled with sincerity. "Remember my promise to you, we don't have to agree on everything, or even anything at all. I will always stand by your side, no matter what." I repeated those same words.

It was true. Nothing could change that. I would stand by Achilles' side through every trial and triumph, our differences only serving to strengthen the bond that held us together, not weaken it.

Chapter 7

<hr style="border-top: 2px dashed;">

The night air carried a chill, causing a shiver to run down my spine. Achilles and I had just completed our fishing excursion, seeking solace next to the crackling campfire we had meticulously constructed outside the mouth of the cave. Despite the presence of a campfire within the sheltering depths of the cave, Lord Chiron insisted that we learn the art of self-sufficiency, requiring us to kindle our own flames in the wilderness.

I sank into the plushness of the grass beneath me, its gentle blades caressing my weary body. Across from me, Achilles positioned himself, his nimble fingers dancing effortlessly across the strings of his lyre. The melodious notes resonated through the night, mingling with the crackling fire, creating a symphony that harmonized with the tranquil surroundings.

"In a world of myths and legends untold, A tale of friendship, brave and bold, With heroes strong, and magic in the air, We'll stand together, a bond we'll share.Oh, stand with me, through the trials we face, In this realm of wonder, our hearts embrace, United we'll be, like a fortress so grand, In this land of dreams, we'll forever stand.From enchanted forests to castles high, Where dragons roam and phoenixes fly, Through treacherous quests, we'll journey far, With each other's strength, we'll reach the stars.Oh, stand with me, through the trials we face, In this realm of wonder, our hearts embrace, United we'll be, like a fortress so grand, In this land of dreams, we'll forever stand.In this realm of magic, where legends reside, We'll face the unknown, side by side, With courage and hope, we'll conquer our fears, In this ancient land, we'll wipe away tears.In the golden age, where dreams come alive, We'll face mythical creatures, and strive, With unwavering faith, and a warrior's might, Together we'll conquer, in this mystical light.Oh, stand with me, through the trials we face, In this realm of wonder, our hearts embrace, United we'll be, like a fortress so grand, In this land of dreams, we'll forever stand.Through the ages, our bond will remain, In this land of magic, our stories sustain, Forever we'll stand, as heroes so true, In this realm of dreams, me and you."

His voice cascaded through the air, a melodious stream that captivated my senses. Mesmerized, I fixed my gaze upon him, my eyes refusing to stray from his face. Every note he sang seemed to weave a spell, enchanting the night with its ethereal beauty.

As the final strains of his song echoed into the stillness, Achilles slowly opened his eyes, meeting my gaze with a tender intensity. A small smile curved his lips, radiating warmth and affection. In that moment, it felt as if the entire world had ceased to exist, leaving only the two of us, connected by the music and the unspoken emotions that danced between us.

"What?" he inquired, his voice laced with curiosity, drawing me deeper into the conversation.

The crackling fire illuminated our faces as I mustered the courage to pose a question that had been lingering in my mind. "Have you ever pondered the notion of giving up all the fighting and glory and just becoming a musician instead." I asked, my words hanging in the air like a delicate melody.

Achilles paused, his eyes reflecting a myriad of emotions. "I have," he confessed, his voice tinged with a hint of wistfulness. "Many times, in fact. But that would be a very boring life don't you think?" A mischievous smile tugged at the corners of his lips, as if he were contemplating the possibilities of such a path.

A chuckle escaped my lips, mingling with the gentle crackle of the fire. "For you, perhaps," I agreed, a shared understanding passing between us. We exchanged smiles, acknowledging the divergent paths that lay before us, yet finding solace in the unspoken connection that bound us in that moment.

A sudden yawn escaped my lips, causing me to stretch my arm languidly, feeling the fatigue of the day seep into my bones.

"I suppose it's time to bid the night farewell," I suggested, rising from my comfortable spot on the grass.

But before I could take another step, Achilles interjected, his voice filled with urgency. "Wait!" he exclaimed, his words cutting through the stillness of the night. "I... I have something for you."

Intrigued, I approached him, drawn by the enigmatic tone in his voice. He patted the patch of grass beside him, a silent invitation for me to join him. With a mixture of curiosity and anticipation, I settled down beside him, the warmth of the fire enveloping us both.

Achilles reached into his pocket, retrieving the wooden dice I had once purchased from the bustling market.

However, they were no longer just ordinary dice; he had intricately threaded a delicate string through them, transforming them into a unique accessory.

"I made this for you," he declared, his voice filled with a mix of pride and vulnerability. His gaze locked onto mine as he extended his hand, silently requesting my arm.

I offered my wrist, feeling a flutter of anticipation as Achilles deftly tied the string around it, the wooden dice now adorning my skin like a cherished talisman.

The weight of the moment settled upon me, leaving me momentarily stunned. I sat there, my eyes fixated on the bracelet, its significance sinking in.

Achilles, sensing my surprise, faltered for a moment, his words stumbling over each other in an attempt to apologize. "Sorry, I should have asked if it was okay to alter your dice. I... I'm such an id-"

Before he could finish his self-deprecating remark, I interrupted him, my voice filled with genuine warmth.

"It's perfect," I assured him, a soft smile tugging at the corners of my lips.

Achilles' expression transformed from shock to confusion as my response registered with him. "You like it?" he repeated, his voice laced with uncertainty.

"I love it! Thank you!" I exclaimed with a grin spread across my face. Without a second thought, I wrapped my arms around him, pulling him into a tight embrace. Achilles released a relieved chuckle, his body relaxing into mine.

But as I held him, memories of my father flooded my mind, a bittersweet reminder from the now turned bracelet dice. The tears that had been threatening to spill over finally broke free, cascading down my cheeks in a torrent of emotion.

Achilles, sensing my distress, cupped my face in his hands, his eyes searching mine for answers. "What's wrong?" he asked, his voice gentle and concerned.

"It... they just remind me of father. I'm sorry," I managed to choke out between sobs. The memories of countless hours spent playing dice with my father, a cherished bond we shared, surged through my mind. It was a cherished pastime that had brought us closer, a tradition passed down from his father to him, and then to me.

Achilles, his eyes filled with empathy, gently wiped away the tears from my cheeks, his touch offering solace in the midst of my emotional turmoil. "There's nothing to be sorry for," he reassured me, his voice tender and understanding. With a comforting embrace, he held me close, allowing me to find solace in his presence.

Grateful for his support, I pulled back slightly from the embrace, my tear-streaked face now adorned with a genuine smile. "Thank you, Achilles," I whispered, my voice filled with sincerity. "It's the best gift I could have ever received."

Chapter 8

It took Achilles a considerable amount of time to unlock the hidden secrets within his spear. He and Lord Chiron dedicated countless hours to unraveling its full potential, and finally, their efforts paid off.

As Achilles explained to me, the spear seemed to merge with him, becoming an extension of his very being. It was as if their thoughts became intertwined, with the spear responding to his every intention. It was both eerie and exhilarating, but Achilles assured me that there was no cause for concern.

On this particular day, we found ourselves standing atop a cliff, overlooking a sprawling forest. The air was still, interrupted only by the occasional melodic chirping of birds.

Lord Chiron and I stood beside each other, a safe distance away from Achilles as he prepared his spear. The golden weapon shimmered in the sunlight, its tip almost caressing his face.

"Are you ready, Achilles?" Lord Chiron inquired.

Achilles remained silent, but his poised stance indicated his readiness. With his free hand pointing towards the horizon, he let out a powerful grunt and hurled the spear forward.

The spear came alive, its surface pulsating with energy as it propelled itself into the unknown. The resounding boom that followed shattered the silence, echoing through the air, as if the very heavens had cracked open.

And then, silence descended once more, as we stood there, eagerly awaiting the return of the spear.

"Stay focused," Lord Chiron instructed, his voice calm but tinged with anticipation and excitement.

Gradually, the sound of the spear's approach reached our ears. Achilles extended his arm, prepared to catch the weapon.

"Get ready!" Lord Chiron exclaimed, unable to contain his excitement.

The sound grew closer, and within seconds, Achilles swiftly spun on his ankle, facing the incoming weapon. With a mighty grip, he caught the spear, his face contorted with effort under the scorching sun. His muscles strained, as if his arms might detach from his body, as he fought to restrain the spear's momentum and prevent it from continuing its journey across the world.

Achilles collapsed to the ground with a thud, the impact reverberated through the earth, sending a cloud of dust swirling into the air while the spear continued its flight through the sky. I rushed to his side, ensuring he was unharmed. Carefully, I helped him to his feet, my hands brushing off tiny rocks and dust that were glued to his his sticky back.

"Are you alright?" I whispered, my voice hushed with apprehension.

"No! I'm not alright!" he exclaimed, his frustration evident. I couldn't blame him; he had been practicing this maneuver for nearly a week, yet he still struggled to control the spear. Achilles was accustomed to excelling at everything, effortlessly mastering any skill. This failure was a new and humbling experience for him.

The resounding boom of the spear's return shattered the silence once more, prompting Lord Chiron to swiftly step forward, his movements fluid and calculated. With a grace that belied his equine form, he intercepted the spear, his hands gripping the golden shaft with unwavering strength. The sound of the booming weapon reverberated through the air, its vibrations pulsating through my body.

Achilles reached out, his fingertips brushing against the cool metal of the spear. With a deft touch, he deactivated its thrusters, silencing the powerful force that had propelled it through the sky.

"You must learn to speak to it, Achilles. If you simply treat it as a weapon it will continue to act like one. I've told you this already." Lord Chiron admonished.

"I know..." Achilles grumbled in response, his voice laced with frustration. The weight of his failure hung heavy in the air, casting a shadow over his usually confident demeanor. I could see the determination etched into his features, his brow furrowed with a mixture of anger and disappointment.

"Go and get yourself cleaned up." Lord Chiron commanded, his voice firm yet filled with concern. Achilles, his body smeared with dirt and sweat, longed to protest, to continue the arduous training that had pushed him to his limits. But before he could utter a word, Lord Chiron turned away, striding purposefully into the distance.

Achilles stood motionless, a solitary figure with his back turned towards me, his gaze fixed upon the distant horizon. The golden rays of the setting sun bathed his figure in a warm, ethereal glow, casting long shadows that danced around him. As I observed him in that poignant moment, an overwhelming urge surged within me - a longing to reach out, to offer solace, and to assure him that everything would ultimately be alright. I yearned to extend my hand, to hold him tightly in a comforting embrace, and to whisper words of reassurance into his ear.

Yet, as my hand tentatively extended towards him, Achilles abruptly turned his head, his gaze piercing through me with a mixture of determination and vulnerability. His voice, tinged with a hint of sorrow, cut through the silence, rejecting any consolation I might have offered. He demanded solitude, even if just for a fleeting moment. Reluctantly, I withdrew, leaving him standing there, a solitary figure amidst the fading light, grappling with his own inner turmoil.

I sat perched by the crackling fire, its warm glow casting flickering shadows across the cave walls, as Lord Chiron diligently stirred the pot, the aroma of the simmering meal wafting through the air. The atmosphere hung heavy with unspoken thoughts, both of us yearning to discuss Achilles and his absence, yet words eluding us.

Finally, breaking the silence, Lord Chiron's voice cut through the stillness. "He will return soon, Patroklos. Do not fret."

My leg twitched with anticipation as I anxiously awaited Achilles' arrival. He had not returned home since I left him earlier, and worry gnawed at my heart. I longed to be by his side, to offer my support, but he had ordered me away, demanding solitude. And so, I sat here, restless and impatient, counting the moments until his return.

"You might as well occupy yourself with something productive," Lord Chiron suggested, his voice filled with wisdom. "Perhaps play the lyre or delve deeper into the study of medicine."

Frustration welled within me, and I couldn't help but voice my inner turmoil. "What is my purpose, Lord Chiron?" I asked, my voice tinged with exasperation. "I have accomplished many things alongside Achilles, but never to the extent of his skill. And now, as Achilles faces failure for the first time in his life, I am consumed by the desire to help him instead of trying to compete against him. You told me that I am more than a mere follower, that my purpose extends beyond serving him. Yet, no matter what, my thoughts always gravitate towards him. Even when he frustrates me or surpasses me in every endeavor, I still yearn to be with him, to stand by his side. So, what if my purpose is to serve him? Because I cannot help but want to be there for him, always." The words spilled forth without thought, my heart guiding their path.

Lord Chiron regarded me for a brief moment, a knowing smile slowly spreading across his face. "You have yet to realize it, young one?" he said, his voice resonating with authority. "You are not meant to simply serve him. You are meant to be with him. He is not your Lord, but your friend, your brother, the other half of your very soul." His words struck me with profound force, their truth resonating deep within my being.

I sat there, stunned by Lord Chiron's words, my mind racing as I tried to process their meaning. He was right. Achilles was more than just a master to me; he was my closest friend, my confidante, and my soulmate. We had been through so much together, our bond unbreakable, forged through shared experiences and a deep understanding of one another.

My heart ached with longing as I yearned to be reunited with him, to feel his presence beside me once more. I wanted to run outside and search for him, to call out his name until he appeared before me. But Lord Chiron's interruption brought me back to reality.

"Now, if you don't mind," he said, gesturing towards the ingredients laid out on the table. "Care to prepare the salad?"

I nodded, grateful for the distraction, and set to work, my hands moving mechanically as I chopped and sliced the vegetables.

The night was dark and quiet, save for the crackling of the campfire and the distant sound of crickets. I sat by the fire, staring at the empty seat across from me, where Achilles should have been. Lord Chiron had cautioned against venturing out to search for him, assuring me that we would begin the search at first light if Achilles had not returned by then.

But I couldn't bear the thought of waiting. The mere idea of Achilles being in danger or distress gnawed at my heart, overriding any sense of obedience. I longed to be by his side, to feel his touch, hear his voice, and bask in his presence. So, I defied Lord Chiron's instructions and set out to find Achilles.

Leaving the campsite, I made my way towards the cliffs where Achilles had been training earlier that day. The wind whipped at my hair, and my heart raced with anticipation. As I approached the edge, my heart skipped a beat. There, standing motionless, was Achilles himself. It was as if time had frozen, preserving him in the exact spot where I had last seen him.

Desperation clung to the air as I called out Achilles' name, my voice carrying the weight of my concern. In that moment, it was as if the very essence of his being had transformed. He spun around, his features illuminated by the soft glow of the moon. His eyes, usually filled with joy and playfulness, now shimmered with unshed tears. The sight tore at my heart, fueling an urgent need to hold him close.

Without a second thought, I lunged towards him, my arms enveloping his trembling form. I clung to him as if our embrace held the power to halt the world's destruction. His voice, choked with emotion, broke through the silence.

"Patroklos..." he sobbed, his words heavy with self-doubt. "I am nothing but a failure."

The words struck me like a dagger, piercing my soul. I refused to let his spirit be crushed by such thoughts. With unwavering conviction, I reassured him, my voice brimming with unwavering faith.

"No, you're not Achilles!" I declared, my words infused with unwavering belief. "You will accomplish this. You are Achilles of Myrmidon, capable of conquering the world itself. And I will be there, every step of the way. When you fall, I'll help you rise. We'll do this together."

As I positioned myself behind Achilles, my fingers moving gently over his, a surge of energy coursed through me. It was as if the very essence of the spear he held came alive, vibrating with an intensity that resonated deep within my being. In that fleeting moment, it felt as though the weapon possessed a consciousness of its own, as if it had thoughts and emotions that I could somehow comprehend.

As our hands connected, a profound connection formed between us and the spear. It was a silent understanding, a shared language that transcended words. It was as if the spear and I were in sync, our intentions aligned, and we both knew what needed to be done.

Achilles, his focus unwavering, readied himself, his gaze fixed upon the distant horizon. With a sense of purpose and determination, he gripped the spear tightly, his muscles tensing in anticipation. In that moment, our hands intertwined, I leaned in closer, my voice a gentle whisper in his ear.

"Together," I murmured, my words carrying a depth of conviction and unity.

"Together," Achilles echoed, his voice filled with resolve and trust. And with that single word, we became a singular force, a harmonious blend of strength and restraint.

With synchronized precision, we propelled the spear into the vast expanse before us, its trajectory guided by our united effort.

The resounding boom of the spear's departure gradually faded, leaving behind an expectant silence. We braced ourselves, eagerly awaiting its return. As the spear drew nearer, Achilles reached out, his hand poised to grasp it. Yet, as his fingers closed around the weapon, it trembled within his grasp, as if resisting his touch. The strain on his face was evident, his grip faltering under the weight of the spear's restless energy.

Reacting swiftly, I interlaced my fingers with his, my grip firm and unwavering. I could feel the tremors coursing through the spear, a reflection of Achilles' own struggle to control it. Sensing the urgency of the moment, I spoke, my voice laced with a deep understanding.

"It is not merely an inanimate object," I explained, my words carrying a profound truth. "It is alive, and it senses your intentions. Do not force it to stop, but rather, communicate with it. Speak to it, soothe it, and let it understand you."

Achilles, his brow furrowed with uncertainty, grappled not only with the challenge of halting the spear's vibrations but also with the vulnerability required to forge a connection with it. In this world, Achilles allowed himself to be vulnerable with only one person, and that person was me.

"Approach it as you would approach me," I advised, my voice gentle yet steadfast. "Speak to it as you would speak to me. Close your eyes and let thoughts of me guide your words."

Achilles obediently shut his eyes, his features relaxing as he surrendered himself to the task at hand. Miraculously, the tiny thrusters surrounding the spear retracted, their persistent hum fading into silence. The once-agitated vibrations stilled, as if acknowledging Achilles' effort to establish a connection. In that moment, it was as if the spear recognized him, accepting his presence with a newfound calmness.

Achilles, his eyes wide with astonishment, slowly opened them, taking in the sight before him. A radiant smile spread across his face, mirroring the elation that surged through his being. Without hesitation, he enveloped me in a tight embrace, his arms encircling me with a strength that conveyed his gratitude and affection.

As he pulled away, we stood there, our gazes locked, the world around us fading into insignificance. In that moment, it was as if time had ceased to exist, and all that mattered was the profound connection between our souls. There was an unspoken language that flowed between us, transcending the need for words. It was a language of understanding, of shared emotions and thoughts that intertwined our very beings.

With our hands still clasping the spear, the energy between us intensified. It was as if our touch amplified the connection, merging our essences into one harmonious force. In that moment, we became a singular entity, united not only in purpose but in spirit.

No words were necessary, for we could feel what the other felt. Every emotion, every intention, every ounce of love and determination coursed through our intertwined souls. It was a profound merging of two individuals, bound together by a force greater than ourselves.

Our lips met with a hunger that had been building between us for what felt like an eternity. It was a gentle collision, a tender exploration of each other's mouths. The taste of anticipation lingered on our tongues as we melded together in a passionate dance.

It was impossible to discern who initiated the kiss, for in that moment, our desires merged into one. The world around us faded away, leaving only the sensation of our lips moving against each other, caressing and teasing. We were lost in a sea of sensations, drowning in the intoxicating rush of pleasure.

As our hands roamed, they traced the contours of our bodies, mapping every curve and dip. Fingers brushed against heated skin, igniting a trail of fire wherever they roamed. A desperate need to connect physically consumed us, driving us to explore every inch of each other.

We sought solace on the rugged terrain, where we placed our garments beneath us. Our bodies intermingled and limbs intertwined, as we endeavored to unite our souls on a physical plane.

The synchronized motion of our bodies transformed into a harmonious symphony of longing, building in intensity with every breathless gasp and passionate moan. We were completely consumed by a mutual sense of urgency, driven by an insatiable desire to reach the pinnacle of pleasure in unison.

As our bodies moved with raw passion, a symphony of ecstasy played out. The world around us blurred into a haze of pure sensation, where nothing existed except the touch of skin, the warmth of breath, and the electric currents that surged between us.

In the climax of our fervent union, the spear we had held so tightly slipped from our grasp, tumbling to the ground with a resounding thud. The spell of our love trance was shattered, and the outside world slowly began to seep back into our consciousness.

Overwhelmed by the intensity of our emotions, my body was left exhausted, yet my mind was alive with the lingering sensations that echoed through my thoughts. As I surrendered to the blissful embrace of sleep, a sense of profound beauty washed over me, knowing that I had experienced something truly transcendent.

Chapter 9

S ince that unforgettable night, a profound transformation had taken place. Me and Achilles, against all odds, had forged an unbreakable bond that seemed to defy the laws of nature. Our connection, once strong, had grown even stronger, intertwining our lives in a way that seemed impossible.

Despite this remarkable change, everything else remained unchanged. We continued our rigorous training under the watchful eye of Lord Chiron, honing our skills to perfection. We had reached a point where there seemed to be nothing left to learn, or so I believed.

On this momentous day, Lord Chiron made an announcement that sent ripples of anticipation through our beings. Tomorrow, we would be departing for our respective homes, marking the end of our time here. Today, he declared, would be our final lesson, one that would teach us the essence of peace.

As we stood before him, Lord Chiron's gaze held a mixture of wisdom and sadness. He spoke of the importance of cherishing this day, of spending these precious moments together and creating lasting memories of tranquility and solace. It was a bittersweet reminder that our fate beyond this sanctuary remained uncertain.

Achilles, ever driven by his insatiable thirst for glory and immortality, clung steadfastly to his aspirations. It was his purpose, his very essence. And yet, a part of me couldn't help but yearn for a different path for him. Now that our relationship had blossomed into something beautiful and profound, I couldn't help but hope that he might consider relinquishing the relentless pursuit of legend for a life of peace.

We lay on the lush grass, surrounded by the enchanting embrace of the deep forest. Above us, a myriad of ambrosia fruits dangled from the branches, their vibrant hues contrasting against the verdant canopy. With our hunger gnawing at us, we had plucked a couple of the fruits to satisfy our hunger. The fruit resembled pomegranates, but they were as soft as peaches and had sweet pear-like juices.

I can still recall the first time I looked at the vast forest and noticed the abundance of ambrosia. It stood out prominently, as if it didn't belong. However, every time we explored, we could only find a few of them.

As I savored the succulent taste of the ambrosia, Achilles tenderly ran his fingers through my unruly hair. We had not had a haircut in months, and despite our pleas for Lord Chiron to cut it, he repeatedly reminded us that he was not a barber. Our ultimate resolution was simply to cut them using knives, resulting in our hair becoming disheveled and uneven.

"Anything you wish to do?" Achilles inquired, his voice filled with genuine curiosity.

I pondered his question for a moment, relishing the tranquility of our surroundings. "No," I replied softly, "simply lying here with you is more than enough."

Achilles, however, brimmed with an infectious enthusiasm. In one swift motion, he sprang to his feet, disrupting the serene ambiance that enveloped us. "We've been here for a year, and we've barely scratched the surface of this forest. Today, being our last day, I propose we embark on an exploration!" His eyes sparkled with anticipation, his excitement palpable. Even after all this time, I marveled at how effortlessly he transitioned from calm to exuberant.

I couldn't help but jest, "So your plan for today is to get lost and get eaten by wolves."

Achilles laughed, his voice brimming with mirth. "Come on! It'll be an adventure, and besides, there won't be any wolves. When was the last time you saw any dangerous creatures here? Never! Since we arrived, we've encountered only herbivores. Isn't that a bit suspicious?"

Achilles was right. As he voiced his thoughts, the peculiarity of our encounters with only herbivorous creatures became increasingly apparent. The absence of any dangerous predators in this vast and untamed forest was indeed strange.

"You are right. It is quite strange." I replied, scratching the back of my head. "Do you think...maybe Lord Chiron, has something to do with it? Maybe we're inside some sort of perimeter he's set and it's safe. He is an excellent hunter after all, and he does know the woods by heart."

Achilles' eyes gleamed with excitement, his impatience palpable. "Whatever the reason, I want to explore! Let's go!"

We embarked on a seemingly endless journey, the forest enveloping us in its labyrinthine embrace. The towering trees stretched endlessly into the horizon, their branches intertwining like a complex web of nature's tapestry. With each step, the air grew thicker, the scent of moss and earth mingling with the sweet fragrance of wildflowers. It felt as if time had become irrelevant, lost amidst the ethereal beauty that surrounded us.

As we ventured deeper, a peculiar sensation washed over me. It was as if the trees themselves were guiding us, their branches arching and bending in a deliberate manner, as if beckoning us forward. The forest seemed alive, pulsating with an unseen energy, and my instincts screamed that we were being watched. Goosebumps prickled along my arms, a shiver coursing through my spine.

I asked him if the trees appeared to be guiding us, but I didn't fully grasp the absurdity of my statement until I vocalized it. Surprisingly, Achilles didn't dismiss my concerns or accuse me of hallucinating; instead, he agreed with me.

The realization sent a chill down my spine. We were not alone in this forest; there was an unseen force guiding our path. The thought both exhilarated and unnerved me.

Our journey continued, the forest gradually thinning until we stumbled upon a small clearing. My heart sank as I beheld the sight before me. The ambrosia fruits, the very ones we had consumed earlier, lay scattered on the ground, their vibrant hues contrasting against the earthy backdrop. Confusion and dread washed over me, intertwining in a tumultuous dance.

"Is that..." I managed to utter, my voice trembling with a mixture of fear and disbelief.

Achilles' eyes widened in recognition. "It is," he whispered, his voice filled with a strange mix of excitement and wonder "This is awesome!"

I stared at him, unable to comprehend his reaction. How could he find joy in this inexplicable occurrence?

"Are we certain we haven't simply wandered in a circle?" I desperately grasped for a rational explanation. "Or perhaps an animal stumbled upon the ambrosia and brought it here, to a place that somehow bears a striking resemblance to our previous location."

"Or..." Achilles paused, a mischievous smile playing on his lips, his voice trailing off as he savored the moment, "it's magic."

I scoffed dismissively. "There's no such thing as magic."

Achilles looked at me, his eyes filled with a mix of amusement and disbelief. Swiftly, he unsheathed his gleaming spear, holding it before me with reverence. "And what is this?" he asked, his voice tinged with a hint of challenge. "This is magic, right here. You tell me you don't believe in that?"

I shook my head, my voice resolute. "That was crafted by the greatest blacksmith to have ever lived. It's not magic, Achilles. It's technology, a result of skilled craftsmanship and scientific understanding."

Achilles stared at me in shock, his eyes searching mine for a glimmer of understanding. "Of all the people in this world, I never would have expected you to be so rational when it comes to magic."

"It's not about being rational," I replied firmly. "It's about seeking the truth, understanding the reasons behind the extraordinary. There is always an explanation, even if we do not yet comprehend it."

Achilles grinned, a mischievous twinkle in his eyes. "Ah, I see what's happening," he exclaimed, his voice filled with a mix of amusement and triumph. "The mysteries of this forest have unsettled you, and you're desperately trying to rationalize them away. It's all right, my friend. I won't tell Lord Chiron that you were spooked by a few trees."

"I was not spooked!" I protested, my voice rising in frustration. The words came out louder than intended, and I immediately regretted them, feeling a pang of disappointment in myself. "I'm simply trying to make sense of it all. There must be a reason why we find ourselves back in this exact spot."

Achilles simply shrugged, his gaze wandering back to the enigmatic trees. "Magic," he stated simply, his voice filled with an unwavering conviction.

With a heavy sigh, I resigned myself to the fact that I couldn't sway Achilles in this matter. The forest had unsettled me, and my attempts to rationalize the inexplicable were futile. Achilles, on the other hand, seemed to revel in the mystery, his excitement undeterred by my skepticism.

Achilles's enthusiasm was infectious, his eyes gleaming with excitement as we pushed forward into the depths of the forest. Time and time again, we found ourselves inexplicably back at the very spot we had started from. It was as if the forest itself conspired against our progress, thwarting our every attempt to venture deeper into its mysterious depths.

Achilles bounded towards Lord Chiron with uncontainable excitement, his eyes alight with curiosity and anticipation. His rapid-fire questions poured forth like a torrential downpour, seeking answers and insights into the mysteries that enveloped the forest. But to our dismay, Lord Chiron remained stoically silent, his gaze filled with a tinge of sadness and a hint of reluctance.

It was evident that Lord Chiron possessed the knowledge we so desperately sought, yet he chose to withhold it from us. His refusal to engage in our inquiries only deepened the enigma that shrouded the forest, leaving us feeling both frustrated and intrigued. It was as if he held the key to unlocking the secrets of the woods, but was unwilling to share it with us.

The night air was crisp and cool, the stars twinkling brightly overhead as we sat by the crackling campfire. Achilles lay sound asleep beside me, his chest rising and falling with each deep breath. But for me, sleep was elusive, my mind racing with a thousand thoughts and worries.

Anticipation swirled within me as the thought of tomorrow's journey back home filled me with excitement. However, a sense of unease gnawed at the edges of my mind, casting a shadow of worry over the horizon of the unknown future that awaited me.

The events of the day still lingered in my mind, sending shivers down my spine. The strange occurrences we had encountered had left me feeling uneasy, and the thought of sleeping outside only heightened my paranoia.

Suddenly, the sound of twigs snapping shattered the peaceful silence, causing my heart to race with fear. I scanned the surrounding darkness, straining to see what had caused the noise, but my eyes were useless in the blackness.

Achilles's hand on my shoulder jolted me from my panicked thoughts. "What's wrong?" he asked, his voice laced with concern.

"I...I heard something," I stammered, my voice trembling with fear.

"Don't be scared," he reassured me, pulling me into a warm embrace. His words were like a soothing balm to my frayed nerves, and I felt my body relax against his. "I'll protect you."

As we lay back down, I could feel his protective presence beside me, his steady breaths a calming rhythm that lulled me into a sense of safety. I never once heard his breathing grow heavy with sleep, and I knew that he had stayed awake, watching over me until I too drifted off into a restless slumber.

The next morning, as the sun began to cast its golden rays upon the forest, we gathered our belongings and prepared ourselves for the journey back home. The atmosphere was heavy with a mixture of emotions, and a silence enveloped us as we walked, each lost in our own thoughts.

Finally, Lord Chiron broke the stillness, his voice carrying a weight of finality. With a deliberate pause, he announced, "This is it. This is farewell."

Achilles stepped forward, his voice filled with confidence and gratitude. "It has been an honor to learn from you, Lord Chiron. I will carry the skills you have imparted to me into battle and make you proud."

Lord Chiron's hand rested on Achilles's shoulder, his eyes filled with a mix of pride and expectation. "Young Achilles," he began, his voice tinged with a hint of nostalgia, "your father is one of the greatest men I know. I have no doubt that you will use the knowledge and skills I have taught you to achieve great things. Do not disappoint me, young one."

Achilles stood tall, his determination shining through. "I will not disappoint you, Lord Chiron," he declared, his voice resolute and filled with pride.

Then, Lord Chiron turned his gaze towards me as Achilles continued onward, his hand finding its way to my shoulder. The weight of his touch carried a sense of trust and responsibility. "Young Patroklos," he said softly, his voice filled with a mix of fondness and wisdom. "I have taught many students before you, but you are unlike any of them. Your search for love sets you apart."

I listened intently, my heart swelling with gratitude for his words.

"Because of this," Lord Chiron continued, his voice carrying a hint of secrecy, "I trust you with a secret. Ambrosia... it is the name of my late wife. She passed away before you were born, and I brought her body here to be buried in this forest she loved. She was also an Olympian, and it is her presence that has given rise to the ambrosia trees. This is why they only grow here in Myrmidon, why their fruits possess healing properties, and why people often get lost trying to reach this place."

I stood there, stunned by the revelation. Everything suddenly made sense, but it took a moment for it all to sink in. Lord Chiron's wife, a goddess, still lived on through the ambrosia trees. It was her guiding presence that had protected us, ensuring we did not get lost or harmed. The absence of dangerous animals and Lord Chiron's unwavering confidence in our safety suddenly became clear; it was because his wife watched over us.

"Why are you telling me this?" It was only question I could ask. Lord Chiron never talked about his past nor the forest so why the sudden change of heart.

He took a moment, his eyes filled with a mix of caution and determination. "Because I trust you with the truth," he replied. "If word were to spread that this forest is the heart of the ambrosia trees, human greed would know no bounds." His anger flickered briefly, but he composed himself, his gaze steady.

"Thank you for your trust, Lord Chiron. I will not betray it," I responded, my voice filled with passion and determination.

Lord Chiron's smile was filled with wisdom and reassurance as he spoke, "Now, set forth, young one. Your journey has just begun."

And so, with newfound knowledge and a sense of purpose, Achilles and I ventured homeward, carrying the weight of the forest's secrets and Lord Chiron's trust with me. Our lives had been forever changed, and we embarked on our respective paths, ready to face the challenges that awaited us.

Chapter 10

As we arrived at our home, we were greeted with a lively atmosphere of feasting and celebration. King Peleus, in honor of his son's return, had organized a grand party and extended invitations to all the kingdoms of the Greek world. However, amidst the excitement, Achilles couldn't help but feel a pang of sadness. His mother, who held great significance in his life, was absent once again, and there was no information about her return. Although Achilles concealed his disappointment, I could sense the hurt he felt deep inside.

As the radiant sun gradually descended, casting a tranquil darkness across the sky, Achilles and I prepared ourselves in our private chamber. We meticulously adorned ourselves in elegant attire, paying careful attention to every detail. Achilles donned a striking white fustanella, a traditional Myrmidon garment that gracefully draped over his thighs. Its loose-fitting sleeves cascaded down his arms, revealing a glimpse of his hands. To complete his ensemble, he wore a resplendent golden vest, embellished with delicate black accents. Meanwhile, I dressed in a similar fashion, with a distinguished dark blue vest adorning my attire. Together, we presented ourselves in a manner befitting the grandeur of the occasion.

"So, how do I look?" Achilles stood before me, his arms outstretched, proudly displaying his meticulously chosen attire. His eyes searched mine, a hint of uncertainty flickering within them.

I couldn't help but suppress a grin, attempting to maintain a composed facade. His anxiousness was endearing, and I found myself chuckling softly at his self-doubt.

"Is it bad?! I knew I should have chosen the red one!" He muttered to himself, lamenting his choice of outfit. I couldn't help but chuckle at his antics.

His gaze shifted back to me, a single eyebrow raised inquisitively. With a gentle smile, I reassured him. "You look more than good, Achilles. In fact, I dare say Lady Helen may pale in comparison."

Achilles blushed, a rosy hue spreading across his cheeks, adding a touch of warmth to his already striking features. "You've already used that line on me you know."

"I know." I replied, closing the distance between us as I approached him "But that doesn't make it any less true."

Drawing him into an embrace, I wrapped myself around Achilles, feeling the strength of his arms encircle me in a protective hold. The sweet scent of ambrosia fruit, reminiscent of divine indulgence and our time together away from home, enveloped my senses, intoxicating and comforting all at once. I nestled my head against his chest, feeling the soft press of his lips and nose against the crown of my head, a tender gesture that filled me with a sense of belonging. His hands, firm yet gentle, grasped my back, providing a sense of security and affection.

Our enthralling moment was abruptly interrupted by a resounding knock that reverberated through the room, shattering the stillness. Startled, we immediately disentangled ourselves from each other's embrace, our hearts racing with a mix of anticipation and trepidation.

As the door swung open, a servant, dressed in a meticulously tailored uniform, stepped into the room. Their eyes darted respectfully between us, their demeanor a delicate blend of deference and duty. With a voice that carried a hint of urgency, they delivered their message, their words hanging in the air like a weighty secret. "The King is awaiting your presence, Your Majesty," they announced, their voice tinged with a subtle tremor of reverence.

With a swift nod of acknowledgment, the servant swiftly retreated, leaving us momentarily alone once again. Achilles, his gaze fixed upon me, seemed to convey a silent understanding. Without uttering a single word, he extended his arm towards me, an unspoken invitation that I readily accepted without a moment's hesitation.

With a confident stride, Achilles led me through the grand corridors of the palace, his hand firmly clasping mine. The walls were adorned with intricate designs, and the floors were polished to a gleaming shine, reflecting the flickering light of the chandeliers that hung above us.

As we approached the dining hall, the sound of chatter and laughter grew louder, and the air was thick with the aroma of delicacies being served. The double doors loomed before us, and as we pushed our way through the throngs of people, we were met with a sea of elegantly dressed guests, their eyes darting towards us with curiosity.

Achilles' presence seemed to command attention, and as we made our way through the crowd, people moved apart, creating a path for us to walk through. The friendly smiles and warm greetings that greeted us made us feel like we were among old friends.

Suddenly, the room fell silent, and all eyes turned towards the head of the table, where King Peleus sat. As soon as he noticed us, he stood up from his chair, his regal presence commanding respect and admiration. With open arms, he welcomed us, embracing us both warmly, a gesture that spoke volumes about his affection for us.

"Ah, my beloved sons!" King Peleus exclaimed, his voice filled with genuine pride and affection as he kept us enveloped in his warm embrace. His eyes sparkled with paternal joy as he took a moment to admire our impeccable attire, his words echoing through the hall.

Aware of the hushed anticipation that had settled upon the gathered guests, King Peleus raised his voice, projecting it with regal authority to capture the attention of all.

"My sons," he began, his voice resonating with a mixture of admiration and reverence, "have emerged from their arduous training with a wealth of knowledge and skills that are known only to a select few. Tonight, I have gathered all of you here to not only celebrate their triumphant return but also to envision a future that holds even greater prosperity for all our kingdoms!"

As his words hung in the air, King Peleus raised his glass, filled with the divine elixir of ambrosia, a symbol of immortality and abundance. The room erupted in a chorus of clinking glasses, followed by cheers and applause that reverberated through the hall, a testament to the shared excitement and hope that filled the hearts of all those present.

Achilles, his voice laced with a hint of concern, leaned in closer to his father, his words intended for only us to hear. "Father, what of Sparta? Have they not yet arrived?" His inquiry carried a sense of anticipation, his gaze searching the room for any sign of their presence.

With a sigh of disappointment, King Peleus lowered himself back into his seat, his regal posture unwavering. "No, my son, they have not graced us with their presence," he replied, his tone tinged with a hint of annoyance. "And to make matters worse, they have not even bothered to send a message. It seems Agamemnon's notorious lack of manners has rubbed off on his brother as well."

In an instant, a spark ignited in the king's eyes, illuminating his face with delight, prompting him to rise from his seat with a new-found energy. Curiosity piqued, I followed his gaze, my eyes landing upon a figure that had captured his attention - Deidamia, a familiar face from the past. It had been years since I last saw her, and yet her presence still held a certain allure. Her golden curls cascaded down her shoulders, framing a face adorned with striking emerald eyes that glimmered like precious gems.

"Deidamia! How lovely to see you!" The king's voice resonated with genuine warmth as he enveloped her in a warm embrace, planting kisses on both her cheeks in a display of affection. "Is your father not accompanying you? I had expected to see him by your side." His eyes scanned the room, searching for any sign of her father, a mix of curiosity and concern evident in his expression.

"No, my gracious King," she responded with a gentle grace, her voice carrying an elegant and sweet tone. Her eyes, filled with sincerity, met Achilles' gaze, prompting a soft smile to grace his lips.

"Achilles," King Peleus addressed his son, a glimmer of mischief in his eyes. "Why don't you honor our delightful guest with a dance?"

"Of course," Achilles replied, his voice laced with a subtle tenderness. He delicately took her hand in his, leading her towards the center of the room where couples had already begun to sway to the music. While I suspected Achilles may have been feigning his enthusiasm for the dance, I couldn't help but feel a twinge of jealousy at the sight of them together.

As the future king, it was imperative for Achilles to secure a marriage and ensure the continuation of his lineage through the birth of an heir. Deidamia, with her exquisite beauty and the close ties between their families, seemed to be the ideal candidate.

While it was not unheard of for individuals to enter into same-sex marriages, the reality remained that, as a member of the royal family, Achilles carried the weighty responsibility of securing an heir. Despite the acceptance of diverse relationships, the necessity for a successor loomed over him, a duty he could not evade, particularly due to his royal status.

It was the one role that Deidamia could fulfill for him, a role that I, despite my affection for him, could not. The realization left me feeling disappointed in myself, even though I knew deep down that there was nothing I could do to change the circumstances.

"Aren't they just perfect for each other?" he King inquired, turning to me with anticipation.

"Absolutely." I replied, concealing my disappointment and offering a false affirmation.

"I never thought you'd lie to me, Patroklos." The King remarked, catching me off guard. I gazed at him, speechless, as he continued. "Ever since you and Achilles returned, I've noticed a subtle shift in your gaze towards him. It may not be overt, but it's enough for me to perceive." He smiled knowingly.

My attempts at forming words faltered, leaving me speechless and uncertain of how to navigate the conversation.

The King, perceiving my struggle, continued with a compassionate tone. "I understand that Achilles may not have an interest in Deidamia. However, as the future King, he carries the responsibility of producing an heir. Please know that his duty does not diminish his love for you."

"I understand." I replied, gratitude lacing my words, as we continued to observe Achilles and Deidamia twirl around the ballroom floor with effortless grace. Their movements were fluid, as if they were two halves of a whole, perfectly in sync with each other. The soft glow of the chandeliers cast a warm light on their faces, highlighting the joy and contentment that radiated from them. Despite my own feelings of disappointment, I couldn't help but appreciate the beauty of the moment.

Deidamia and I stood at the water's edge, feeling the warm sand seep between our toes as the rhythmic ebb and flow of the ocean mesmerized us. The moonlight cast a gentle glow upon us, illuminating Deidamia's radiant blonde hair, which shimmered like Achilles' own.

As we gazed out at the vast expanse of the ocean, Deidamia turned to me, her eyes curious. "So, we've both known Achilles for most of our lives, yet we've only had the chance to meet a few times. How come?"

I pondered her question for a moment, my gaze shifting to the distant horizon. "When he visited you, I wasn't allowed to come. And you didn't frequent this place often either." I shrugged.

She nodded and let out a small hum, seemingly content with my response.

"And how long have you been together?" Her words hung in the air like a heavy weight, catching me off guard.

"How do you know that?" I asked, surprised by her sudden question.

"He told me," she replied calmly, her voice maintaining its soft and caring tone. "He told me while we danced." Her words flowed effortlessly, revealing a depth of understanding that surprised me. "Honestly, I'm not surprised. You two have known each other for so long, and I always sensed that his interest in me wasn't genuine. I'm just glad he's found someone as kind-hearted as you."

Expressing gratitude, I replied, though with a hint of scepticism, "Thank you, but you don't really know me."

Unexpectedly, she let out a chuckle, interrupting the conversation. "Actually, I do. He simply couldn't stop talking about you throughout the entire evening."

Those words echoed in my mind, creating a resonance that stirred a flutter of excitement within me. Achilles had been incessantly discussing me with someone. Although I couldn't quite fathom the reason behind it, the mere thought evoked a delightful sensation akin to a swarm of butterflies dancing in my stomach.

"So," she inquired, her curiosity piqued, "may I ask how long you two have been together?"

I hesitated for a moment before answering, "Quite a while now. Although, I'm not entirely certain if we can truly consider ourselves as being together. It's more like we've been going with the flow without actually discussing the nature of our relationship."

"Trust me, you most certainly are," she assured with a light chuckle, and for a brief moment, we found solace beneath the tranquil night sky, the gentle lapping of waves soothing our spirits. However, her tone soon shifted, becoming more serious than I had ever heard it before. "I'm going to assume you know about mine and Achilles' plan?"

"Yes," I replied, my voice barely above a whisper, conveying my acquiescence to her query.

She gazed at me intently, her eyes probing mine, seeking confirmation of my comprehension of the significance of their plan. "And you do realize how crucial it is?" she pressed, her tone serious and unwavering.

I nodded firmly, my resolve unwavering. "Yes, I do," I affirmed, my voice steady.

Her next question was more pointed, more direct. "So you won't stand in Achilles' way? You won't try to dissuade him from carrying out his duty?" she asked, her voice tinged with a hint of apprehension

"I won't," I said firmly, meeting her gaze with unwavering determination. "He needs an heir, and you are the one who can provide him with one. It's as simple as that," I stated, my words resolute and unwavering.

"Doesn't it bother you?" she inquired, her voice laced with a hint of sweetness, as if she were trying to gauge my true feelings.

"It does," I admitted, my voice tinged with a hint of melancholy. "But as Achilles' sworn companion, it's my responsibility to assist him in making wise decisions, not just for himself but also for his kingdom. I cannot allow my emotions to cloud my judgment or distract me from my duty," I explained, my words measured and resolute.

"I'm glad to hear that," she replied, a smile spreading across her face. "Now I understand why Achilles holds you in such high regard. You possess an inner flame that's hard to describe, but when you speak, your words are filled with passion," she remarked, her tone admiring and appreciative.

"May I ask you something?" I questioned, my voice tentative. "Does it not bother you that your sole purpose in Achilles' life is to bear his child?"

She turned her gaze towards the vast expanse of the horizon, her hair fluttering slightly in the wind. For a moment, she remained silent, lost in thought, before finally responding. "Scyros was once a poor and insignificant island before King Peleus took it over," she began, her voice tinged with a hint of nostalgia. "We used to produce furniture and household items, but the quality was abysmal. However, when the King arrived, he didn't deprive us of our freedom or force us to work for him. Instead, he recognized our potential and provided us with the resources we needed to create masterpieces. And look at where we are now. We have never thrived like this before, and we have become the greatest carpenters in all of Greece. The palace where you reside, my father built it with his own hands. And even though I was born after our island began to prosper, my father never forgot to remind me of how much the King has done for us," she explained, her voice filled with gratitude and reverence.

"So, you are undertaking this responsibility out of a sense of indebtedness?" I asked, my voice tinged with curiosity.

She turned her gaze towards me, her eyes reflecting a mixture of gratitude and determination. "Yes," she replied, her voice filled with sincerity. "I owe my entire life to the King. Without his intervention, my family would have languished in poverty, and perhaps I would never had been born. By fulfilling my duty to bear Achilles' child, we not only strengthen the connection between our families, but we also gain even greater power and influence," she declared, her voice growing resolute. "I cannot disregard the debt I owe to King Peleus, and this is the minimum I can do to repay him for all he has done for us."

In that moment, I couldn't help but feel a surge of admiration for her unwavering loyalty and recognition of the profound role that King Peleus had played in shaping their lives. It was a testament to the power of gratitude and the lengths one would go to honour the debt owed to someone who had irrevocably altered the course of their existence.

As the night progressed, an icy chill descended upon the atmosphere, causing a shiver to run down my spine. The darkness seemed to intensify, casting an eerie ambiance over the surroundings. It was amidst this chilling backdrop that I caught sight of Achilles emerging from the shadows along the shore.

A mischievous grin played upon my lips as I couldn't resist the urge to taunt him. "Did you enjoy your leisurely stroll by the beach?"

Achilles returned my banter with a smirk, his eyes gleaming with amusement. "Indeed, I did," he replied, his voice laced with a hint of satisfaction. "And how are you two getting along?" he inquired, referring to the newfound camaraderie between myself and Deidamia.

We exchanged nods, silently acknowledging the bond that had formed between us. Achilles couldn't help but break into a smile, his approval evident in his expression. However, our moment of tranquillity was abruptly shattered as one of our soldiers approached us with a sense of urgency, his footsteps quick and resolute.

"Your Highness!" he exclaimed, his voice filled with urgency. "The King demands your immediate presence!"

I turned to Achilles, a sense of foreboding settling in the pit of my stomach. Though I was unaware of the details, a deep intuition told me that something was gravely amiss.

Chapter 11

Achilles and I stood beside King Peleus in the dining hall, the atmosphere heavy with anticipation. The lively feast had come to a halt, and a palpable silence enveloped the attendees who eagerly awaited the unfolding events.

Before us stood the formidable Kings of Sparta, their presence commanding respect and attention. It was clear that they carried a weighty and solemn message.

"You heard correctly, King of Myrmidon," King Agamemnon's voice resonated throughout the room, its authoritative tone capturing everyone's attention. "My brother's cherished wife has been cruelly seized by those filthy Trojans!" As his words echoed through the hall, a wave of murmurs rippled among the guests.

"Helen has been taken?" King Peleus exclaimed, his voice laced with shock. "How did this happen?"

"Just yesterday, we had a peace treaty," King Menelaus revealed, his tone filled with bitterness. "They deceitfully signed it, only to brazenly steal my beloved wife from right under our noses! This affront to me and our kingdom shall not go unanswered! It is a declaration of war, and we beseech your kingdom's aid!" Menelaus spoke with a fiery mix of fury and fervor, his words seething like molten lava, his hands trembling as he gestured emphatically.

The murmurs swelled in response to the mention of war. It had been years since the last one, despite the perpetual hostility between Sparta and Troy. And now, after the hard-fought peace treaty that countless individuals had striven for, it seemed that everything would descend into violence and carnage, all because of one woman.

"When do you intend to commence this war?" King Peleus inquired.

"It has already begun," King Agamemnon answered tersely.

"Tomorrow, we shall set sail for Troy," King Menelaus declared, his voice brimming with determination. "With your airships, we anticipate no issues with travel. And as for you, dear Athenians," he turned towards them, "we understand that war is not your forte, but if you provide us with 500 of your impeccable ships, we shall reward you with half of the treasures within Troy." The guests gasped in astonishment. Troy was the wealthiest kingdom outside of Greece, and earning half of its riches would make Athens immensely powerful, perhaps even more so than our own kingdom.

Menestheus, the King of Athens, gulped the piece of turkey he was eating and responded with a simple. "Done."

As a kingdom that governed through democracy, he did not have the authority to make such a decision on his own. However, no one would fault him for accepting the offer. It would be sheer folly to decline.

"And what do you require from me, Kings?" King Peleus inquired.

Myrmidon had alliances with every kingdom within Greece, which meant that if any of them were attacked or went to war, they would have to come to their aid, and vice versa.

"Your unstoppable army of Myrmidons, as many as you can spare, of course." King Agamemnon stated. "And the same goes for your airships. With those on our side, victory will be swift and certain!"

King Peleus contemplated the demands for a moment before finally agreeing. "I will provide you with 500 of my finest warriors and 300 airships. I believe that should be sufficient resources for you to secure victory in this war."

"Excellent," King Agamemnon responded, bowing theatrically.

"But let me pose this question," King Peleus continued. "How do you plan to breach their defenses? The shield has been blessed by Apollo himself."

He raised a valid concern. That impenetrable shield had never faltered, serving as the very reason why they were the most formidable kingdom.

"That is indeed a challenge," King Menelaus acknowledged, only for Agamemnon to interject. "But with your son's spear, we will surely find a way."

All eyes immediately turned to Achilles and then back to the King, awaiting his response.

"You want my son to join you?" King Peleus asked, his voice filled with grave concern. "He is simply too young to fight in a war alongside you."

"I will go," Achilles interjected. "I'll aid you in your war."

"Achilles!" King Peleus exclaimed in frustration. The weight of the decision hung heavily in the air, and I could sense the tension between father and son.

"Very well. It is decided then. I'll send you the meeting coordinates. We'll be seeing you tomorrow." King Agamemnon declared with an exaggerated wave, before he and King Menelaus exited the hall.

I observed King Peleus conversing with Achilles, but the words exchanged were inaudible to me. My thoughts were consumed by the realization that Achilles had agreed to go to war, and I would be compelled to join him as well.

In King Peleus's private office, Achilles and his father continued their heated argument, their voices filled with frustration, echoing through the room.

"You are too young to go and fight in a war, Achilles!" King Peleus yelled, his concern evident.

"If I refuse, it would bring shame upon our Kingdom. As its future King, I cannot allow that to happen," Achilles stood his ground with determination.

"If you go to this war, you won't return as the future King, but as a dead Prince," King Peleus spoke with a deep mix of anger and melancholy.

"Then what was all the training for, Father!? I am more than capable of fighting in this war and bringing glory to both our kingdom and my name. If you were so certain we would lose, why did you readily send away 500 of our men? Are you willing to sacrifice Myrmidon sons to uphold a pact, but not your own?" Achilles questioned, his voice filled with frustration.

"I would sacrifice my entire kingdom to save you!" The King yelled, defending his stance. "Both of you." He turned his gaze towards me, bringing me into the conversation.

"No!" Achilles burst out suddenly. "Don't involve him in this. I have made up my mind, and I am going. I won't allow your paternal emotions to destroy everything you have worked so hard for." Achilles stormed out of the room, slamming the door behind him.

King Peleus sighed, rubbing his face and beard wearily. "Everything I have worked for has been for you..." He spoke solemnly, hunched over the desk.

His eyes met mine, and I could see the tears he desperately held back, glistening in his eyes.

"You have to stop him, Patroklos. You are the only one he will listen to," he pleaded.

"He won't listen to me. He has already made up his mind," I replied, my voice filled with resignation.

"The Spartans believe they can win because they have support from all of Greece. But they won't," the King explained. "Troy's shield will not fall. It never has and it never will. This war will only lead to pointless slaughter. It's not that I don't believe in Achilles's skills, but this war is unwinnable."

"King Agamemnon said that the spear could help defeat the shield. Don't you think so?" I asked, searching for a glimmer of hope within his sparkling eyes.

"Both the spear and the shield were created by the Gods. If there is anything that can bring it down, it would be the spear. But the issue is that none of us know how, and neither does Achilles. The entire plan is based on hope and luck." King Peleus explained, his voice laced with uncertainty.

I took a moment to lower my gaze, contemplating the weight of King Peleus's words. He was right - venturing into battle without a clear strategy would be a perilous endeavor, driven solely by blind hope. It felt like a suicide mission, and perhaps I could find a way to convince Achilles to reconsider his decision to join the war.

"I'll talk to him." I declared. The King's eyes sparked with a glimmer of hope, and a grateful smile graced his face as he placed his hand gently on my shoulder, expressing his gratitude.

Achilles lay on his bed, his muscular frame relaxed but his mind clearly preoccupied. His eyes were closed, but the tension in his brow betrayed his restless thoughts.

"Have you come to dissuade me?" he spoke softly, his voice tinged with a mix of weariness and anticipation.

"Maybe I did, or maybe I just came to sleep since we share the same room," I joked, and a sweet grin appeared on his lips. I fell onto the bed beside him, placing my head on his chest as his arm wrapped around me. "Your father told me that Agamemnon has no plan, and he's right. It all hinges on hoping that your spear might do something, but if it doesn't, then that's it. We lose, and we die."

"My spear will work," he said with certainty. "We didn't spend all that time training just to doubt my skills. I now know how to control the spear to its fullest potential. We will win this war with ease."

"It's still too big of a risk. I mean, what if you don't bring down the shield? What if you die? What will happen to Myrmidon then?" I questioned him, ensuring he considered all the possible outcomes.

With a playful tone, he asked, "Do you seriously doubt my judgment this much?"

"You didn't answer me." My response was stern, and he abruptly rose to his feet, turning his back to me. The weight of his thoughts seemed to hang heavily in the air, and after a brief pause and a heavy sigh, he finally spoke.

"Death. The answer to all of them is death," he said, his voice low and grave. "If the shield stands, then we die. And if we die there will be no future for Myrmidon. Unless I leave an heir to rule..." Silence fell between us. If we were to embark on war the following day, tonight was his sole opportunity to conceive a child.

Achilles turned around slowly to face me, and I couldn't bring myself to meet his gaze. The weight of the impending decision hung heavily in the air, and my voice came out as barely a whisper.

"You are going to do it tonight?" I asked, my words filled with a mix of disbelief and resignation.

"Yes," he replied simply, his voice tinged with a hint of awkwardness. "I already told Deidamia. I just had to tell you before...we did it."

The gravity of his words hit me like a punch to the gut and a surge of frustration welled up within me.

"So...you did think of everything then. You're truly not going change your mind about this?"

There was a small pause before he answered, his voice filled with determination. "No."

A wave of anger washed over me, the frustration bubbling to the surface. "So your solution to this is to go to war and if you die, leave a baby behind for a mother to raise on her own, instead of just staying here and living a happy life?"

"Why are you making this so much more difficult!" Achilles raised his voice, a hint of exasperation creeping in. "You always knew that this was the life I wanted. That this is what makes me happy."

He was right, and I knew it. This was the path he had chosen, the path that brought him joy. But the thought of him leaving a child behind without a father because of his own selfish desires was something I never expected from him.

"You're right!" I snapped, my anger boiling over. "But I would have never expected you to leave a baby behind with no father because of your selfishness!"

His face registered shock, his body frozen in place. My words had struck a nerve, and I could see the hurt in his eyes.

"I-" he began, attempting to find the right words, but I cut him off, unable to bear the weight of the conversation any longer.

"Don't bother! Just go to her and do what you have to do." My voice dripped with contempt as I turned abruptly, slamming the door behind me as I stormed away.

My father had left me all alone when he died, consumed by his own pursuit of glory and honor. Seeing Achilles make the same choice, abandoning his own child for the sake of his ambitions, was a betrayal that cut deep. I couldn't stop him from having that baby, nor could I prevent him from going to war. But I would make sure he understood the grave consequences of his choices, consequences that would haunt him for the rest of his days.

Chapter 12

Last night was a restless one, plagued by a torrent of emotions that made it nearly impossible for me to find any solace in sleep. As the morning dawned, I sought refuge in various activities to distract my troubled mind.

I began my day by engaging in rigorous training exercises, honing my skills on training dummies with a focused determination. Seeking respite from the physical exertion, I turned to the medicinal books bestowed upon me by Lord Chiron, immersing myself in the knowledge they held. Yet, even amidst these scholarly pursuits, my thoughts remained consumed by the tumultuous emotions swirling within me.

Seeking solace in nature, I made my way to the palace gardens and settled beneath the towering ambrosia tree. Its branches swayed gently in the morning breeze, as if in harmony with the melancholic melody that flowed from my fingers on the lyre. The sky above was veiled by dark clouds, lending an air of serenity to the atmosphere. However, within that tranquility, a sense of profound loneliness permeated my being as I reminisced about the countless moments Achilles and I had shared beneath this very tree.

Despite my best efforts to suppress my thoughts of Achilles, they proved to be an insurmountable force. Anger and resentment coursed through me, compelling me to distance myself from him. And yet, I found myself unable to quell the yearning that tugged at my heart. I longed to feel his presence, to taste the sweetness of ambrosia on his lips, and to intertwine our fingers as I played the lyre, accompanied by the melodic timbre of his voice.

A part of me clung to the hope that he would appear, seeking reconciliation and offering an apology. Knowing myself all too well, I knew I would readily forgive him in an instant. And so, I sat there for what felt like an eternity, waiting for his arrival that never came.

Then, out of the corner of my eye, a figure emerged from the distance, golden hair billowing in the wind. My heart skipped a beat, and my body instinctively rose to greet the approaching presence. However, as I fully registered who it was, my excitement waned, replaced by a profound sense of disappointment.

It was Deidamia, making her way towards me with a wave of her hand. I forced myself to reciprocate the gesture, harboring no ill will towards her, but acutely aware that she was not the person I longed to see.

She greeted me, and I returned the greeting, the ensuing silence hanging awkwardly between us. Finally, she broke the silence, her voice cutting through the tension.

"How are you feeling?" she asked, her delicate smile betraying her concern.

"Amazing," I scoffed, my frustration seeking an outlet, even though she bore no responsibility for it.

"So, you haven't spoken to him then?" she inquired, her voice gentle and understanding.

"No, why?" I replied, my curiosity piqued.

"He's at the beach. You should go talk to him," she advised, her words delivered with a tenderness that only served to exacerbate my guilt for scoffing at her earlier.

And so, I found myself at the beach, observing Achilles as he gracefully wielded his spear, as if engaged in a battle against an unseen foe. I watched from a distance, my gaze fixed upon him, until he finished his display and turned towards me. In an instant, his radiant smile illuminated his face, captivating my attention entirely.

"Deidamia said you wanted to talk," I began, my voice tinged with a mix of anticipation and apprehension.

"I do," he affirmed, plunging his spear into the sand. Achilles' piercing blue eyes locked onto mine, holding me captive. "I won't have the baby," he declared with unwavering conviction.

A whirlwind of confusion and relief swept through my mind as I struggled to comprehend the implications of his statement. What did this mean for him, for the kingdom, for Deidamia, for me?

"You're... not having the baby? But why?" I asked, my voice revealing a mix of curiosity and concern.

"Because you were right. It wouldn't be honorable for me to leave a child and its mother behind if I were to perish in battle. I refuse to carry such a burden on my conscience in the afterlife," he explained, his words resolute.

"So, you're still going to war," I stated, my question more of a confirmation, for I already knew the answer. At this point, I was merely acknowledging the inevitable.

"I am," he affirmed, his conviction unyielding.

"Having the baby and staying here to live a peaceful life isn't a good option for you?" I choked on the words, my voice trembling with emotion.

Achilles looked at me with a mix of determination and sadness. "You already know this... I'm not made for a peaceful life, and I definitely won't abandon the war after I willingly chose to join it. It would be humiliating."

His words struck me like a dagger to the heart, and I fought to compose myself. "You are right. I know you won't change your mind, even for me." There was a deep sorrow in the back of my voice as I said that, but I cleared my throat and pulled myself together. "I can't change you, no matter what I do, and it truly frustrates me so much! And yet, I can't stop wanting to be with you... why is that?" I asked, a weak smile forming on my lips.

"My good looks?" Achilles quipped, his smile reflecting all the happiness in the world.

I couldn't help but chuckle under my breath at his comment, grateful for the momentary respite from the heaviness of our conversation. I gazed down at the sand beneath my feet, lost in thought.

Unbeknownst to me, Achilles had moved closer, and our hands were now only inches apart. The tension between us was palpable, a delicate dance of longing and restraint.

"I'm glad you chose not to have the baby," I whispered, my voice barely audible above the crashing waves.

Achilles's eyes locked onto mine, his gaze filled with a mixture of relief and regret. "Me too," he murmured, his voice barely a breath.

As our hands inched closer, the sound of a thundering engine shattered the tranquility of the moment. We both turned our heads to the sky, witnessing the passing of an airship. The sheer power and magnitude of the sound sent shivers down my spine.

The deafening roar of the engine reverberated through the air, shaking the very ground beneath our feet. The airship, a colossal behemoth of metal and power, sliced through the sky with an imposing presence. The sound alone was enough to send chills down my spine, a foreboding reminder of the impending storm that awaited us.

Silently, we exchanged a knowing look, the unspoken understanding passing between us. There was no need for words - the time for contemplation had passed. It was now a time for action, for steeling ourselves for the battles that lay ahead.

Chapter 13

As the airship approached Troy, a sense of anticipation filled the air, causing both the vessel and its occupants to tremble. Just moments ago, King Agamemnon had relayed the plan through the telecoms. Our fleet of 50 airships would support the naval and ground troops in attacking the towns and villages, while the remaining ships, including our own, would lead the charge on the main city.

Directly assaulting the city was out of the question due to the enormous shield protecting it. Instead, our objective was to lay siege, cutting off any means of escape until either a way to break the shield was discovered or the enemy surrendered out of desperation and hunger.

It was a sound plan, far superior to relying solely on Achilles and his spear.

Suddenly, the warning light flashed red, and the pilot's voice crackled through the speaker. "E.T.A. 1 minute. Prepare for jump."

Everyone rose to their feet and assumed their positions. Achilles and I stood at the front, his voice resonating with power, authority, and unwavering confidence.

"Many of you have fought in countless wars, while many, like myself, are new to this. But regardless of where we are in our journeys, we are all brothers! So lets fight united in bringing even greater glory and honor to our kingdom!" Achilles' words were met with resounding cheers from our comrades, even those communicating through the telecoms.

The excitement and adrenaline coursing through the air were palpable, infecting everyone, including myself. It was a mixture of exhilaration and fear. Not only were we facing the very real possibility of meeting our demise, but a small part of me reveled in the thrill of it all.

The back door of the airship creaked open, and the sound of the thrusters grew louder.

Achilles glanced at me, awaiting my approval, and I nodded. With a swift motion of his gauntlet, his golden armor materialized, its brilliance shining in the dim light.

Equipped with our own armors, we followed Achilles as he leaped out of the airship.

The wind whipped against my face with an aggressive force as I descended through the sky. My heart pounded even harder as the adrenaline surged through my veins.

The city sprawled out before me, its immense size visible even from this height. It dwarfed our entire kingdom, planting a seed of doubt within me about the success of this audacious attack.

As the ground rushed closer and closer, I deployed my parachute, jolting my body as the sudden force of air resistance and gravity collided.

The ground loomed ominously, and I feared that I might miss my landing and break every bone in my body. The feeling of dread intensified, causing my breathing to become erratic and my vision to blur.

Just as I believed this descent would end in disaster, Achilles' voice echoed through my comm.

"Patroklos! You're descending too quickly!" His voice brimmed with genuine concern.

"I-I don't know how to slow down! Achilles, what do I do?!"

"Stay calm and listen to me! Grip the handles tightly and push down. Just like we practiced!" His instructions rang in my ears, and I followed them as best I could, pressing down on the handles while silently praying to the Gods for protection.

Within seconds, my speed began to decrease, and I managed to land on the ground, rolling forward until I finally came to a stop. My armor had shielded me, though I was certain that I had accumulated a fair share of bruises.

Achilles landed gracefully beside me and immediately rushed to my side.

"Are you alright?!" he shouted, his concern evident as he checked my body for any signs of injury.

I couldn't help but smile and replied, "Yes."

He pulled me into a tight embrace, a gesture that would have lasted indefinitely if we weren't in the middle of a war zone.

Fortunately, our entire troop landed safely, though a few suffered injuries during the descent. Falling through the sky wasn't a skill that had been extensively taught to us, except for the seasoned soldiers, of which we were fortunate to have many.

Our airships positioned themselves strategically around the city, and simultaneously, their speakers blared King Menelaus' message.

"I am King Menelaus, and I bring the full wrath of Sparta, supported by the naval might of Athens and the formidable fighters of Myrmidon and their airships." King Menelaus spoke with unwavering confidence, a hint of anger simmering beneath his words. "You started this war by stealing my beloved wife and breaking the peace treaty! Surrender my wife, your kingdom, and your people, and we may just show you mercy."

We stood motionless, our eyes fixed on the imposing city before us, waiting for a response to King Menelaus' ultimatum.

And then, it came...

The ground trembled beneath our feet as the city's defenses sprang into action. Canon balls drenched in flames erupted from every corner of the city walls, hurtling towards our airships with deadly precision. The air crackled with tension as the projectiles streaked through the sky, their fiery tails leaving trails of smoke in their wake.

But our airships were not defenseless. In a display of technological prowess, their automated defense systems activated, unleashing a barrage of countermeasures. Missiles erupted from the airships, creating a dazzling display of light and sound as they intercepted the incoming canon balls. Explosions blossomed in the sky, the deafening booms echoing across the field as the threats were neutralized.

The silence settled over us once more, and we stood there, anticipation building as we awaited the arrival of the Kings. Time seemed to stretch on, and in the hours that passed, we managed to construct a modest camp. It wasn't much for the 500 of us, but it provided some semblance of comfort.

In the distance, we caught sight of flickering lights steadily approaching. Finally, King Menelaus and King Agamemnon had arrived. Their presence brought a sense of relief and hope to our weary hearts.

"My dear friends, thank you for your unwavering patience," Agamemnon beamed, gracefully dismounting his horse. He was accompanied by King Menelaus and a multitude of their soldiers. "We have successfully captured all the towns, and we are currently establishing our camp in the nearby temple of Apollo."

"It seems that our plan is progressing smoothly. All that remains now is the shield," Achilles declared, his gaze fixed on his spear, filled with determination as he extended it to its full length.

Taking his stance, Achilles prepared himself, his spear pulsating with power as its thrusters came to life. With a deep breath, he launched the spear towards the shield.

Sparks flew and energy erupted from the point of impact, captivating our attention. Then, like a bolt of lightning, the spear shot up into the sky.

To our astonishment, the shield remained unscathed, not a single scratch marred its surface. Wide-eyed and mouths agape, the soldiers were witness to technological marvels and divine tools unlike anything they had ever seen before.

Undeterred, Achilles extended his palm, summoning the spear back to him. He continued to charge and shoot it at the barrier, over and over again, but the result remained unchanged.

Achilles let out a frustrated grunt and hurled the spear once more, but the outcome remained disappointingly the same.

"Well... that is disappointing," Agamemnon sighed, his gaze falling upon the rocky ground.

"No! I can do it!" Achilles yelled, his anger palpable.

"There is still tomorrow, my child," Menelaus spoke with compassion, a stark contrast to his previous anger. It was both interesting and weird to hear him speak this way; he almost sounded like a concerned father.

"My brother is right. We should head to the temple and rest there until tomorrow. We will keep the airships on guard. You mentioned they can remain airborne for weeks without refueling, correct? I do not want them bombarding us in our sleep, with their little toys." Agamemnon suggested, his voice filled with mockery.

Achilles was too consumed by his anger to respond, so I nodded on his behalf, acknowledging the plan. And so, we made our way towards the temple of Apollo.

As we followed behind the Kings, I whispered to Achilles, attempting to offer reassurance. "We will figure it out. We always do." I smiled and reached for his hand, which initially tensed into a fist but gradually relaxed under my touch.

The camp was not far, a mere twenty-minute walk on foot. Upon arrival, we found Spartan troops diligently setting up tents, and provisions were being distributed among the weary soldiers.

Among them were Trojan civilians being held captive. Some complied willingly, while others futilely resisted. It pained me to witness their suffering, but I felt powerless to intervene.

Suddenly, a young soldier hurriedly approached us. "Hello, Prince Achilles and Lord Patroklos! King Agamemnon has assigned me as your assistant."

Achilles and I exchanged glances, both raising an eyebrow in confusion.

Achilles was perplexed by the sudden appearance of the boy, while I was still grappling with the fact that he referred to me as "Lord." No one had ever addressed me in such a manner, and it felt strange, to say the least.

"Please inform your King that we appreciate his hospitality, but we do not require a mere errand boy," Achilles spoke dismissively, ready to walk away. I quickly grabbed his arm, stopping him in his tracks.

"What is your name?" I asked, my tone sweet and gentle.

"I am Eurypylus," the chestnut-haired boy replied, his head hanging low.

"And what exactly is your role as our assistant?"

"Anything!" he exclaimed, a sudden burst of energy animating him. "I will do anything you ask! Please, just don't send me back to Lord Agamemnon. He will think I am useless." Tears welled up in Eurypylus' eyes, and I immediately placed my hand on his shoulder, guiding him along.

"Come, you can show us the way to our tent."

Eurypylus eagerly ran ahead, leading the way with a wide smile plastered across his face.

"You seem to have a way with children," Achilles commented, observing my interaction with Eurypylus.

"He appears to be no older than thirteen. How can they subject someone so young to this?" I exclaimed, my eyes widening in disbelief.

"That's just how Spartan society operates," Achilles explained. "They start training them from the moment they can walk." The notion of children being subjected to such intense military training from such a tender age seemed utterly absurd.

"That's ridiculous..." I whispered, my gaze shifting from Achilles to the young boy. A mixture of horror and sadness filled my heart as I desperately hoped that it was merely a rumor. Yet, there he stood, living proof of the harsh reality.

It had been a week since our arrival in Troy, and we were still no closer to victory. Achilles' spear had failed to penetrate the enemy's defenses, forcing us to resort to plan B: wait until they surrendered from starvation.

Every day, Achilles tirelessly hurled his spear at the shield for hours on end, despite the futility of the exercise. I stood by and watched, offering silent support through my mere presence.

Time seemed to crawl by at an agonizingly slow pace. Our days were spent playing games or training with each other, but the monotony of it all was beginning to wear on us.

As the sun began to dip below the horizon and Achilles' energy waned, we prepared to return to camp. Suddenly, the loud sliding of the gates being opened caught our attention. Three figures emerged from the distance, two men and a woman. The woman was Helen, her golden hair cascading over her shoulder, and her eyes as blue as Achilles'.

"Summon the Kings of Sparta," the older of the two men declared. "The sons of Troy wish to speak."

Chapter 14

We all gathered beneath the night sky, a thick blanket of clouds obscuring the moon, casting an eerie darkness over us. The air was heavy with the scent of impending rain, a dampness that clung to our skin and mingled with the tension that crackled in the atmosphere.

As I looked around, I could sense the palpable anger emanating from each person present, as if it were seeping through their pores. The weight of their emotions hung in the air, making it almost difficult to breathe.

"Finally decided to engage in conversation?" King Agamemnon was the first to break the silence. "Is that perhaps due to your arms feeling heavier than usual? Your legs more difficult to move? Or is it the painful sound of hunger rumbling in your children's bellies?"

"We are not on the brink of starvation, if that's what you assume," the older man, presumably Prince Hector, retorted with his head held high. "We possess ample sustenance and vegetation to sustain us indefinitely."

"Enough of this insolence!" Menelaus bellowed, his voice filled with fury. "Step forward and face me like a man, you coward! How dare you steal another man's love!"

Before either of the brothers could respond, Helen's voice interjected, cutting through the tension. "Menelaus, you have been a wonderful husband. You have given me more than I deserve. You have been loyal where other husbands have not. But we both know that our marriage was not founded on true love."

Tears streamed down Menelaus' cheeks as his lips quivered with emotion.

"My love was true..." He whispered. "Did you truly not love me?"

"I did," she replied, placing her hand against the barrier that separated them. "I do, but not in that way. I believed that what I felt for you was true love, until I met Paris. When I saw him, I realized that this is truly how I should feel. I'm sorry for the pain I've caused you, and I know that I can never repay you for the wonderful years that you have given me. But I implore you, all of you, to end this war and return home."

Agamemnon scoffed and chuckled. "You truly believe that we would simply retreat because you willingly went with them? They still violated the treaty."

"They violated it because of me, so I plead with you to forgive them. If you seek someone to blame, then blame me. Take me back if that is your true desire. Do whatever you wish with me. Just spare these people, for they are not to be held accountable."

"This is my responsibility as well," Paris interjected. "I was the one who convinced Helen to accompany me. The fault lies with me, but I implore you to leave us in peace."

"Perhaps..." Menelaus spoke softly. "Perhaps we should just depart."

"Have you forgotten what he has done to us, brother?!" Agamemnon seized his brother by the shoulder and gestured towards Paris. "He stole your wife! He brought humiliation upon you, me, and our entire kingdom! Do not let him rob you of your pride as well. Face him in combat! If this is truly your fault, young Prince, then duel my brother. The victor shall claim Helen."

Menelaus underwent a sudden transformation, his demeanor changing drastically. His brother's words had kindled a fire in his eyes, making them blaze with an intense fervor. He growled out a challenge, demanding a duel.

Paris, on the other hand, seemed to be at a loss for words. He stood there, caught in between Helen and his brother, Hector. The tension in the air was palpable as Hector and Helen tried to dissuade Paris from fighting against Menelaus.

Agamemnon whispered something to his brother, possibly concocting a plan or inciting him further. Meanwhile, Achilles and I watched the scene unfold in front of us.

Achilles' face was inscrutable, his features as cold and unmoving as stone. I nudged him, trying to get a read on his thoughts. Achilles' gaze flickered towards me, but his expression remained enigmatic.

Curiosity getting the better of me, I inquired, "What are you thinking?"

Achilles, known for his openness with me, replied, "Nothing." The unusual secrecy in his response hinted at a deeper disturbance troubling him.

Concern etched across my face, and I pressed further, "What's wrong?" I asked again.

"I said it's nothing," he responded with a touch of forcefulness, signaling his desire to keep his thoughts concealed.

Respecting his need for privacy, I made the decision not to pry any further. If the matter held significance, Achilles would confide in me when he felt ready.

As the anticipation grew, we observed Menelaus and Paris preparing for their duel. From a distance, we watched intently as the shield slowly opened, allowing Paris to step onto the battleground. I couldn't help but wonder how he managed to do such as a thing. However, before I could ponder further, Menelaus lunged at him, brandishing his sword with fierce determination.

In a swift motion, Paris skillfully evaded Menelaus' attack, dodging his sword with agility. With his shield raised, Paris deflected the subsequent onslaught of strikes, desperately trying to ward off the relentless assault from the seasoned warrior. Menelaus showed no mercy, denying the young Prince any opportunity to gather his thoughts or react strategically.

Yet, as the battle wore on, Menelaus began to show signs of exhaustion. Paris, ever vigilant, seized the moment, swiftly side-stepping and delivering a well-aimed jab to Menelaus' shoulder. A chorus of gasps and murmurs erupted from the troops behind us, their astonishment mirroring our own. The sight of their King being stabbed froze Paris in place momentarily. Regrettably, the wound proved to be superficial, fueling Menelaus' rage even further, as he charged at Paris once again.

The clash between the two combatants intensified, with Menelaus launching a flurry of wild thrusts while Paris struggled to defend himself, his movements limited to mere blocks. Each blow from Menelaus pushed Paris further and further backwards, until he stumbled and fell, leaving himself vulnerable to Menelaus' impending strike.

The tension in the air was palpable, as Menelaus prepared to deliver the fatal blow. However, in a moment that seemed to defy fate, an arrow pierced through the already injured shoulder of the King, causing him to stagger backward. The collective weight of the fall seemed to reverberate through our very beings, as if we ourselves were the ones crashing to the ground.

My eyes darted in search of the source of the arrow, and to my astonishment, it was Hector who had unleashed the shot. With unwavering determination, he rushed to his brother's aid, swiftly lifting him up, and together they sprinted towards the open barrier, leaving us all in a state of awe and disbelief.

"Kill them!!" Agamemnon's shrill command pierced the air, sending a shiver down my spine. The thunderous sound of countless footsteps reverberated through the ground as the troops behind us surged forward, their determination palpable.

Reacting with lightning speed, Achilles hurled his spear towards the entrance just as the Princes made their way through. The clash of the spear against the barrier's energy resonated like a deafening explosion, threatening to rupture my eardrums. Yet, undeterred by the cacophony, Achilles sprinted towards his adversaries, his eyes fixed on the unfolding battle, disregarding the lifeless form of Menelaus lying in his path.

With a fierce determination, Achilles seized the spear and exerted all his strength, pushing and pulling in an attempt to create an opening. But to our collective shock, the spear unexpectedly detonated right before him, sending him sprawling to the ground, dangerously close to Menelaus' lifeless body.

Driven by an instinctual surge of adrenaline, my body propelled itself forward, desperate to reach Achilles as swiftly as possible. Panic clouded my mind, as a torrent of worst-case scenarios flooded my thoughts, threatening to overwhelm me.

Finally reaching Achilles' side, I dropped to the ground, my hands trembling as I swiftly removed his gauntlet, peeling away the layers of armor to assess his injuries. Every inch of his body was meticulously examined, my heart pounding in my chest as I searched for any signs of harm.

A mixture of relief and sorrow overwhelmed me as I clung to Achilles, my grip tightening with every sob that escaped my lips. 'He is fine,' I thought to myself, gratitude flooding my thoughts. 'Thank the Gods, the armor protected him!'

Gradually, I felt Achilles' body shift as he regained consciousness, his arm encircling me in a comforting embrace. "Achilles," I choked out, my voice trembling with emotion. "Are you in pain?"

His face, marred by bruises and scratches, managed to conjure a weak smile, a glimmer of resilience shining through. "I'll be fine," he reassured me, mustering the strength to stand on his own. I extended my hand, offering my support, but he stubbornly declined, determined to prove his independence.

"Damn you, Achilles!" I couldn't contain my anger any longer, my voice reverberating with a mix of relief and frustration. "I thought you died!"

Achilles let out a grumble, his gaze piercing through me. "Obviously, I didn't," he retorted curtly, his resilience resurfacing. "You should be more worried about him." He gestured towards Menelaus, who was being carried away by the Spartans.

The fury within Agamemnon erupted like a volcano, his voice booming with righteous indignation. "Damn those treacherous fiends!" he bellowed, his finger pointed accusingly at the city. "They will pay for this!"

Sensing the need to regroup and strategize, I interjected, my voice filled with a sense of urgency. "We should head back," I suggested, my words punctuated by the arrival of raindrops, slowly trickling down our hair. The sky seemed to weep alongside us, mirroring the weight of our emotions.

Back at camp, I delicately pressed a cotton cloth soaked in healing oil against Achilles' split lip. He winced in response, instinctively pulling his head back, but I firmly held it in place, determined to tend to his wounds.

A mischievous glimmer danced in his eyes, a sign that he was ready to unleash one of his trademark quips. "I don't remember Lord Chiron teaching us to be this rough," he teased, his voice laced with a hint of amusement.

I couldn't help but smile, my focus unwavering as I continued to apply the soothing oil to his injured lip. "Well, being nice hasn't been working so far, so I thought I'd try a bit of a rougher approach," I replied, my tone light but tinged with concern. "So, are you ready to tell me what has been bothering you?"

Achilles met my gaze for a moment before sighing in defeat, his vulnerability seeping through his warrior facade. "I don't know how to take down the shield," he confessed, his voice tinged with frustration. "It's the main purpose for why I am here, and if I'm not able to do it, then I'm just useless." He stood up abruptly, turning away from me and leaning against a nearby table, his shoulders slumped with the weight of his self-doubt.

"We all knew that the spear wasn't a guarantee to take it down," I reassured him, my voice gentle but firm. "No one is blaming you for not being able to do it."

"But it's me we're talking about here!" Achilles' voice cracked, his frustration giving way to a deep-seated insecurity. "I'm Achilles, son of the legendary King Peleus, the one blessed with Hephaestus' greatest weapon! I should be able to take it down!"

"And you will," I insisted, stepping closer and placing a reassuring hand on his shoulder. "Just give it time. We'll figure it out together." But as I tried to offer my support, he shrugged off my touch, his resolve hardening.

"Stop with the 'we,' Patroklos," he pleaded, his voice on the verge of crumbling. "This is something I have to do by myself. It's my destiny. I have to ensure that I am worthy of becoming a great hero."

"You are worthy," I whispered, my voice filled with conviction. "You're more than worthy. This war won't define your worth, and neither will taking down the shield."

"But you're wrong," Achilles retorted, his voice filled with a mix of determination and desperation. "This war is the biggest to ever happen. If I take down the shield, I'll be the man who did the impossible. This will be my defining moment."

"Fine, then," I replied, shrugging with exaggerated nonchalance, masking the hurt that welled up within me. "If you don't need my help, then do it alone!"

With that, I stormed out of the camp, my heart heavy with a sense of rejection. Achilles had always been stubborn, but never like this. His obsession with the war and his own worthiness threatened to consume him, and no matter how much I tried, he simply wouldn't listen.

I needed to clear my head, to find solace away from the chaos and the weight of unrequited help. The temple stood before me, its grandeur beckoning me with a promise of tranquility. It was the first place I saw, and without hesitation, I sought refuge within its sacred walls.

Chapter 15

I had visited the temple a couple of times before, but never had I experienced it at night. Stepping inside, I immediately sensed a palpable shift in the atmosphere, as if I had entered a completely different realm.

In the morning, when the first rays of sunlight filtered through the circular glass ceiling, adorned with an exquisite etching of Apollo poised with his bow, the temple took on an ethereal quality. The warm glow illuminated the space, casting a gentle radiance on the intricately carved walls.

However, the temple transformed entirely at night. Moonlight delicately seeped through the glass ceiling, casting a soft, serene glow over the surroundings. The rhythmic patter of raindrops outside added to the tranquility, creating an enchanting ambiance that seemed to transport me to another world.

At the far end of the room, a magnificent marble statue of Apollo stood proudly, clutching a golden sun in his outstretched hand above his head. Its gleaming surface seemed to shimmer in the moonlight, emanating an aura of divine power and grace.

Drawn to the mystical allure of the moonlit scene, I found myself leaning against the cool, stone wall, gazing at the limited amount of moonlight that managed to penetrate the room. The gentle tapping of rain against the glass ceiling lulled me into a state of peaceful contemplation, and before I knew it, my eyelids grew heavy and I succumbed to sleep.

Suddenly, a sound shattered the tranquility, jolting me awake. It was a distinct tapping, but much louder and heavier than the gentle raindrops. Blinking my eyes open, I found myself momentarily blinded by the brilliance of the sunlight streaming through the glass ceiling.

To my utter astonishment, a majestic white crow perched gracefully on the edge of the windowpane. Its feathers were pristine and glistening, like freshly fallen snow. Each movement it made was deliberate and precise, as it repeatedly pecked at the glass with its sharp beak.

I stood there, captivated by the sight before me. Never had I seen or even heard of a crow that wasn't black. This ethereal creature seemed to defy the laws of nature, emanating an aura of enchantment. Its presence felt otherworldly, as if it belonged to a realm beyond our own.

However, before I could even question it, the creature gracefully spread its wings and took flight. Its elegant soaring through the sky left me breathless.

Rubbing my neck, which had grown stiff from leaning against the wall, I rose to my feet. The soreness reminded me of the passage of time, grounding me in reality as I tried to ease the discomfort.

As I prepared to depart from the temple, my eyes caught sight of something peculiar on the floor. An apple lay there, abandoned and out of place. It struck me as odd, for no soldier would waste food.

Curiosity compelled me to pick up the apple and examine it closely. Its vibrant red skin was unblemished, its flesh firm and untainted. Perplexed, I scanned the surroundings, searching for any other signs of scattered items. Yet, there was nothing else to be found. Though intrigued by this enigma, I ultimately decided to leave the temple and dismiss it from my mind.

As I ventured beyond the temple's entrance, the sight of soldiers training in a makeshift ring caught my attention. Their bodies glistened with sweat, their faces etched with determination, as they endured the scorching heat of Troy's unrelenting sun.

Above us, airships passed by, some descending to deliver much-needed supplies from Greece. The back doors of these vessels opened, revealing soldiers who emerged carrying crates to a nearby station. The weekly restocking of provisions was a testament to the insatiable appetites of these men, who consumed rations with immoderate fervor.

Once the soldiers ceased to emerge from the airship, a figure appeared, causing my mouth to drop open and my eyebrows to furrow in confusion. It was none other than Queen Thetis herself. Her piercing gaze locked onto mine, and she approached with an air of urgency.

"Patroklos," she spoke with a tone laced with concern. "Where is Achilles?"

I stumbled over my words, caught off guard by her sudden presence. "I-I'm not sure," I stammered, my mind still reeling from the unexpected encounter. "I haven't seen him since last night. Why are you here, my Queen?"

Her eyes bore into mine, fierce and unyielding. "You're not sure?" she questioned, her voice carrying the weight of disappointment. "You're supposed to be by his side, always! Have you forgotten your oath, child!?"

My gaze dropped instantly, unable to meet her intense scrutiny. The humiliation she made me feel was overwhelming, causing my voice to come out as a mere whisper. "I'm sorry..."

Before the Queen could continue speaking, her words were interrupted by Achilles' voice, filled with surprise and confusion. "Mom!? What are you doing here?"

"I have grave news, my love," she replied, her grip tightening on Achilles' arm as she pulled him away. "We must speak privately."

As Achilles glanced back at me, his expression a mix of curiosity and concern, I quickly averted my eyes, overwhelmed by a sense of shame and cowardice. The exact nature of my emotions remained unclear, perhaps a combination of both

I stood in the middle of the grand temple, its towering marble columns casting long shadows across the mosaic floor. The air was heavy with the scent of incense, and the flickering candlelight danced on the walls. I gently touched the smooth beads of my dice bracelet, a comforting presence against my skin, as Eurypylus sat at a nearby table, diligently practicing his reading.

"We... um, we offer our prayers and... offer-ings to you, seek-ing your di-vine... di-vine guid-ance and pro-tec-tion," Eurypylus stumbled over the words, his brow furrowed in concentration.

"You're doing great! Keep going," I encouraged, my voice filled with genuine admiration.

"May... May your bless-ings... shower upon us like the sun's rays, and may we always walk in your... your radi...radi..." Eurypylus struggled to find the right word, his frustration evident.

"Radiant," I supplied, a smile tugging at the corners of my lips.

"Radiant...footsteps," he finally completed the sentence, a triumphant look on his face.

"Bravo, Eurypylus! You're getting better every time," I praised him, my eyes shining with pride.

"What's the point of this anyway? Shouldn't I be sharpening your weapons or learning to fight? These words will be useless in battle," Eurypylus questioned, his voice tinged with frustration.

"Learning to read and write isn't useless, Eurypylus. It's a necessary skill, and even if you never end up using it, it's still better to have it just in case," I explained gently, hoping to instill the importance of education in him.

The boy sighed heavily, placing the book aside with a dramatic gesture.

"So what's wrong between you and Prince Achilles?" he blurted out, his curiosity getting the better of him.

I was taken aback by his directness, my eyes widening in surprise.

"What do you mean?" I responded, my voice betraying a hint of defensiveness.

"I haven't seen you two together since Queen Thetis' arrival. Every time you pass each other, you don't greet or acknowledge him. I might not know how to read, but I'm not stupid," Eurypylus observed, his tone filled with a mix of innocence and perceptiveness.

"Well..." I sighed, a mixture of emotions swirling within me, my fingers continuing to rub the dice bracelet. "You're right. We just had a disagreement, that's all. Nothing to get too concerned about."

I offered him a weak smile, hoping he would drop the subject. But, of course, he didn't.

"Are you two together?" he asked, his curiosity unabated.

Shocked and uncertain about how to respond, I stood there frozen, my mouth hanging open. The boy looked at me with an arched eyebrow, probably finding my reaction peculiar.

"We..." I stammered, my hand nervously rubbing the back of my head. "It's complicated... I guess."

"Oh, do you not love each other anymore?" Eurypylus inquired innocently, his eyes searching mine for answers.

"Of course we do!" I exclaimed, my voice filled with a mix of passion and frustration. The boy jolted back, clearly startled by my outburst. I quickly regained my composure and continued, my tone softer now. "It's just... Achilles usually never keeps his thoughts from me. He's always so strong and prideful, but when it's just the two of us, he becomes this different person. He's kind and gentle and playful, although sometimes irritating. But I love that about him, and he always tells me everything that's on his mind."

As I spoke, I tightened my grip on the dice bracelet, my longing for Achilles becoming overpowering.

"But recently, he has been distant and wouldn't talk about his feelings. And when I finally got him to talk, he said that he didn't want my help. That he has to ensure he's worthy of all his titles and glory. That he has to take down the shield by himself because it's his destiny. But by doing so, he's made me feel useless. He's pushing me away and torturing himself with this obsession, and it just hurts to watch and not be able to help him." I poured out my frustrations, my words filled with a mixture of sadness and anger.

"I'm sorry..." Eurypylus spoke, his voice tinged with genuine concern. "Perhaps I could make you a drink to cheer you up?!" His eyes sparkled with youthful excitement, his eagerness to help evident.

I couldn't help but smile at his offer, grateful for his presence and unwavering support. Just seeing Eurypylus, with his youthful energy always warmed my heart.

"Thank you, Eurypylus," I replied, my voice filled with genuine appreciation. "That would be wonderful. But remember, after you make the tea, we'll continue with your reading."

The boy let out an exaggerated groan, his shoulders slumping in mock defeat. But deep down, I knew he understood the importance of his studies and that he had no choice but to listen to my command.

Chapter 16

Weeks had passed since our arrival at the temple, and the lack of progress was becoming increasingly apparent. Achilles, consumed by his futile attempts to bring down the shield, had grown desperate. The toll was evident in the dark circles under his eyes, a testament to his sleepless nights spent tirelessly working at the shield.

Inside the temple, Eurypylus and I had created a makeshift home, setting up sleeping bags and transforming the space into a sanctuary from the chaos outside. Despite my offer for him to sleep in the tent, Eurypylus insisted on staying by my side, and I found solace in his company.

As we worked to make the temple more comfortable, Eurypylus asked me a question that weighed heavily on both our minds. "How much longer do you think the war will last?"

I paused, contemplating the grim reality. "Until the Trojans either starve or the barrier falls, and it seems neither is happening anytime soon," I replied, organizing the scattered and torn books on the shelf.

In the process, my gaze caught a glimpse of faint scratch marks beside the bookshelf. I hadn't seen them before, but they made me think of the strange apple and other odd events that had been happening lately. Things were disappearing or being moved around, and there were whispers that I had assumed were merely the soldiers outside causing a commotion.

"Eurypylus..." I spoke softly, not wanting to alarm the boy or alert whoever or whatever might be lurking on the other side of the bookshelf. "Go fetch Achilles."

Confusion filled Eurypylus' eyes as he processed my request. For weeks, I had avoided any interaction with Achilles, avoiding eye contact and keeping my distance. Now, suddenly, I was asking the boy to summon him.

I narrowed my eyes, silently urging Eurypylus to understand the urgency of the situation. My gaze shifted between the mysterious scratch marks and the boy, hoping he would grasp the gravity of the situation.

"Okay..." Eurypylus murmured, his voice tinged with uncertainty. Whether he fully comprehended my unspoken message or not, he dutifully went to fetch Achilles.

A conflicting battle waged within me as I contemplated my next move. Should I attempt to slide the bookshelf on my own, confronting whoever was hidden behind it? Or was it possible that this person posed no threat at all? If they had been stealing our food all this time, why hadn't they simply killed us in our sleep?

Logic dictated that I should wait for Achilles, relying on his strength and presence. It would be the smarter play in this situation. However, another part of me rebelled against the idea of depending on him any longer. At some point, I had to take action and not rely on others for help.

In a moment of either bravery or sheer stupidity, I mustered the courage to push the bookshelf aside. Surprisingly, its weight felt lighter than anticipated, allowing me to reveal a dark hole in the wall behind it. Suddenly, a roar echoed through the space, and a figure charged towards me. Reacting quickly, I sidestepped, causing the person to stumble and fall to the ground.

Before I could fully comprehend who this person was, another figure emerged from the hole, swiftly pinning me down with a blade pressed against my throat. The rust on the blade sent a chilling sensation through me, and the slightest movement could result in a deadly outcome. Desperately, I gripped the person's arm, holding on tightly.

"Brisseis! Don't kill him!" The person on the ground beside me yelled.

"He's going to kill us, Chryseis! We can't let him go!" I realized then that both of them were young women.

The one who held me captive had long, dark hair that cascaded down to my face, gently caressing it. Her eyes were filled with the weariness of restless nights. I could feel the grease on her grip and the pungent stench emanating from her.

"B-Briseis, right... I want to help you!" I yelled, desperately hoping she would believe me.

"Lies!" She screamed. "You should be grateful I didn't slit your throat while you slept after what you did!"

"Briseis! He's just a child!" The other woman's voice softened, attempting to diffuse the tense situation. "We agreed we wouldn't hurt anyone."

"As long as we were safe! We're not anymore!" Briseis retorted, her voice filled with fear and anger.

"You are very right about that Miss." Agamemnon's voice cut through the tense silence like a knife, interrupting the standoff between Briseis and me. He had arrived with his soldiers, and the sight of them sent a shiver down my spine. "If you want a chance to make it out of here alive, then I'd recommend putting the knife away," he advised, his tone dripping with arrogance.

Brisseis turned her attention to him, her knife still pressed against my skin. "You! You are the one who took my Uncle! Where is he!" she screamed, her fear and anger palpable.

"He's probably locked up with the other slaves. You're more than welcome to join him!" Agamemnon taunted, a cruel laugh escaping his lips. His words seemed to ignite a fire within Briseis, and she lunged at him with all her might. But before she could reach him, one of Agamemnon's soldiers swiftly struck her on the head with the back of his sword, knocking her unconscious.

The other girl, Chryseis, screamed in horror and rushed to her friend's side. She was about to meet the same fate, but Agamemnon halted the soldier's attack. Chryseis knelt beside Briseis, cradling her head in her arms, tears streaming down her face. Blood flowed from the wound, staining her hair.

I rushed to her aid at the sight of her bleeding head. Ignoring the pain in my own neck, I tore a piece of my tunic and hastily fashioned it into a makeshift tourniquet. Gently, I tied it around Briseis' head, hoping to stem the bleeding.

Just then, Achilles appeared, pushing through the soldiers with concern etched on his face. "Patroklos! What happened?" he demanded, his voice filled with worry.

"Carry her to the infirmary!" I instructed, my voice filled with urgency. I could hear the soldiers murmuring, likely questioning how and why I had the authority to give orders to my superior.

"Hold on, young Prince." Agamemnon's voice echoed through the temple as he kneeled next to the two girls. "Who are you two? You are dressed quite nicely, if you overlook the dirtiness...and the stench."

The girl, Chryseis, raised her tear-streaked face to meet his gaze and spoke. "We are priestesses of Apollo. I am his chosen, Chryseis."

Agamemnon's eyes lit up with a sinister gleam as he realized the potential leverage he held. "His chosen, you say?" he repeated, a sly grin spreading across his face. "That's it! Hahaha! That's how we'll bring down the shield! A trade, a priestess for a city!"

"Achilles!" I desperately cried out, my voice echoing through the temple. "I can't stop the bleeding, help me!"

In an instant, Achilles sprang into action, swiftly scooping her up into his arms. He was prepared to carry her away to safety, but his path was abruptly blocked by Agamemnon.

"This woman is my slave, Achilles," Agamemnon asserted, his voice laced with a low, ominous undertone. "I haven't given you any orders to take her anywhere yet."

Achilles' response was immediate, his tone mirroring Agamemnon's. "Watch yourself, King of Sparta. I do not take orders from you," he retorted. "Besides, would you rather your slave bled to death?"

"No, I don't," Agamemnon replied, his voice reverting back to its usual tone. His words were laced with a hint of amusement as he continued, "And you know what? Since your companion here was the one to uncover them, I shall grant you the privilege of keeping the girl and doing as you please with her. Consider it my humble apology." With a flourish, he gracefully bowed, his movements infused with his characteristic theatricality.

My heart raced as Achilles and I raced through the camp, our feet pounding against the dirt path. Urgency consumed us, propelling us forward with a relentless determination. The camp buzzed with activity, but we were focused on one thing - reaching the infirmary.

Finally, we burst through the tent, our breaths heavy and labored. Achilles gently cradled the girl in his arms, his touch careful and tender. Her face was pale, her eyes closed, and a blood-soaked tourniquet wrapped tightly around her head. The sight sent a shiver down my spine.

Achilles swiftly moved to a nearby cabinet, his hands searching for the Ambrosia oil. With a sense of purpose, he handed it to me, his eyes filled with trust. I took a deep breath, feeling the weight of responsibility settle heavily upon my shoulders. This was the first time I would be working on a fellow human being, and the gravity of the situation was not lost on me.

Under the watchful eyes of Lord Chiron, I had undergone extensive training for moments like these. I knew the techniques, I understood the procedures, but nothing could fully prepare me for the reality of it all. The thought of working on a living, breathing person filled me with a mix of determination and trepidation.

Carefully, I applied the Ambrosia oil to her wounds, my hands moving with a steady precision. The girl remained still, her body limp and vulnerable. I focused all my energy on the task at hand, blocking out the chaos within my mind.

As I finished, Achilles took over, skillfully bandaging her head. I turned to a nearby washing station, the sound of rushing water soothing my frayed nerves. I washed my hands meticulously, scrubbing away the remnants of the girl's blood, hoping fervently for her well-being.

"She'll be fine," Achilles spoke softly, his voice filled with reassurance as he approached me. "Now...care to explain why you didn't wait for me? Eurypylus said you called for my help."

"I didn't know what was on the other side. I asked him to fetch you in case it was someone dangerous and to keep him safe," I explained, vigorously scrubbing my hands in an attempt to rid them of the stubborn stains.

"And yet, you didn't wait for me. Why?" Achilles questioned, his voice tinged with concern.

"Because I can't always rely on you!" I slammed my hand against the cold metal tub, my frustration boiling over. "You didn't want me to assist you because you felt unworthy. Well, I didn't want your help because I'm tired of constantly depending on you for everything. How can I be your companion when you excel at everything? You're right not to want my help; I'm utterly useless."

"Patroklos..." Achilles' hand gently grasped my face, and a wave of emotions overwhelmed me. In the midst of trying to focus on myself, I had forgotten how much I yearned for his touch. "Where is all this coming from? All I wanted was to prove my own worth by taking down the shield on my own. I never wanted you to feel useless."

His words struck me like a lightning bolt, jolting me back to reality. Had I overreacted? Misjudged his intentions?

"I never minded being lesser than you, but when you said there was no 'we,' it hurt," tears streamed down my face, my voice breaking. "And this war...you're so consumed by it that I'm afraid it's devouring you, and I can't do anything to help because you won't let me."

"You are not lesser than me!" Achilles' hands now cradled my face, gently wiping away my tears. "You are more than I deserve. And you're right about the war; it consumes my every thought. It's crucial to me that I bring down that shield and make a name for myself, especially now." His gaze shifted away from me, and I sensed that his words carried a deeper meaning than just the war.

"What do you mean by 'especially now'? Has something happened?" I inquired, concern etched across my face.

"I..." He hesitated, his eyes filled with sadness. Whatever plagued him was far worse than I had imagined. "I want to tell you...but I don't know if I should."

I could feel the weight of his internal struggle. Whatever it was, he was grappling with a heavy burden.

"It's your choice. If you don't want to share, you don't have to," I assured him, though disappointment lingered beneath my words. I longed for him to let me in, to allow me to help him.

"I'm...I'm..." His words caught in his throat, and I could see the struggle etched across his face. I reached out, taking his hand in mine, offering a gentle smile to mask my own disappointment. I wanted him to know that I was there for him, no matter what.

And then, finally, the words spilled from his lips, but my mind struggled to process them. It resisted, refusing to accept the truth. So, I asked him, needing confirmation, even though I dreaded it.

"What did you say?" I asked, my voice barely a whisper, my heart pounding in my chest.

And his response shattered me.

"I'm going to die."

Chapter 17

"Poseidon talked to the fates for my Mom. They said I'm going to die." Achilles' words hung heavy in the air, as if the weight of his impending doom had settled upon the room. His eyes, once filled with wonder and possibility, now seemed empty and devoid of hope. It was as if the fates themselves had closed off all other paths, forcing him onto this one inevitable journey towards death..

"No!" I yelled furiously, my voice filled with desperation. Achilles jolted in shock, his eyes widening at my sudden eruption. "Because they said you will die, doesn't mean it will happen now. It could be in ten years, or even a hundred from now."

"Patroklos..." Achilles began, but I ignored him, my words tumbling out in a torrent of emotion.

"They- They're playing tricks! Trying to make us fall for these lies!"

Suddenly, my body froze in place, my pacing halted as Achilles seized my movement. I looked into his eyes, searching for a glimmer of hope, but all I found was resignation.

"Patroklos..." Achilles spoke softly, his voice heavy with sorrow. His eyes closed shut, and I felt his head fall against mine.

My own eyes closed, tears welling up and cascading down my cheeks. I couldn't hold back the overwhelming grief that washed over me.

"I can't lose you!" I cried, my voice shattering like glass. My wailing grew more erratic and uncontrollable.

"Patroklos..." Achilles' fingers gently touched my chin, lifting it up. I opened my eyes, meeting his glistening gaze. He had been crying too. "We both knew this was a possibility. We both knew that I could die by coming here. This doesn't change anything, except that I have to bring down the shield before I die or before someone else somehow manages to do so."

"It does change everything!" I choked out, my voice cracking. "Before, it was a possibility, but now it is certainty. I can't bear to lose you too..."

Achilles fell silent, and I stared at him, waiting for him to say something, anything. I wanted him to tell me he was wrong, that he had changed his mind. I wanted him to grab my hand and take me back home, away from this impending tragedy. But all he said was, "I'm sorry."

Those three words hung in the air, heavy with regret and finality. We didn't speak anymore. There was nothing more I could say to him, no words that could change his mind.

Fury and grief consumed me, intertwining in a whirlwind of emotions. I longed to hit him, to release the anger that burned within me. Yet, at the same time, I mourned for him, for the life that would be cut short. But above all, I simply longed for this chaos to end.

I wrapped my arms tightly around Achilles, burying my face in his chest. I cried, my tears flowing freely as if I had already lost him.

What else was I supposed to do? How else was I meant to react to this heart-wrenching situation? I felt utterly powerless, unable to stop him from walking this path towards death. And in that moment, I knew I was going to lose him, just as I had lost my father.

As my consciousness slowly returned, I could hear the sound of shouting in the distance. The emotional turmoil I had experienced had completely exhausted me, causing me to pass out.

As the shouting grew louder, my eyes shot open in an instant. Standing before me was Achilles, with Briseis tightly bound to the bed, desperately struggling to free herself.

"Untie me, you bastard!" Briseis screamed, her voice filled with anger and desperation as she pulled at the ropes.

"Calm down! We're trying to help you," Achilles attempted to soothe her, but he backed away from her wild kicking.

"Where is Chryseis!?" she screamed, her voice echoing through the room. Her eyes were wild with anger, searching for any sign of the missing girl.

I quickly stepped forward, my hands raised in a gesture of surrender. "Hey!" I called out, trying to calm her down. "We mean you no harm. In fact, we're the ones who healed your injury. You were bleeding really badly, and we saved you." I hoped my words would reach her, that she would understand our intentions and be willing to talk.

The woman's gaze shifted between me and Achilles, her anger still palpable. Her face twisted into a terrifying expression, reminiscent of one of the Erinyes. It was clear that she was not to be trifled with.

But then, something unexpected happened. Her eyes locked onto mine, and I could see a flicker of recognition and understanding.

The tension in her face seemed to ease slightly, as if she was considering the possibility that we weren't her enemies after all.

"Why?" she grumbled, her voice heavy with skepticism. "Why would you help me?"

I took a moment to gather my thoughts before answering. "Why not?" I responded, my voice filled with sincerity.

Briseis scoffed, her laughter tinged with bitterness. "You expect me to believe that? That you're helping me out of the kindness of your heart?" Her words dripped with cynicism, as if she had long lost faith in the goodness of humanity.

I stood my ground, refusing to be swayed by her doubts. "Yes," I affirmed, my voice steady and unwavering.

Her face transformed, shifting from a sneer of disbelief to one of confusion. It was as if she couldn't decide whether I was a fool or if I truly believed in the power of compassion. After a silent moment of locked gazes, I noticed her muscles gradually relax on the bed, a glimmer of hope flickering in her eyes.

"Fine, but I'll only talk to you. Get him out of here," she demanded, nodding pointedly in Achilles' direction.

Achilles stood stoically, his arms crossed and his face a mask of indifference.

"Alright," I agreed, knowing that it was important to respect her wishes. But Achilles immediately refused.

"I'm not leaving you alone with her," he stated firmly, his voice leaving no room for argument.

"It's okay," I reassured him, offering a small smile. "She won't hurt me. And besides, she's tied up." I gestured towards the ropes that bound Briseis to the bed, hoping to ease Achilles' concerns.

Achilles was clearly reluctant, but after a moment of consideration, he reluctantly agreed. With one final glance in my direction,
he exited the room, leaving me alone with Briseis.

The atmosphere in the room grew increasingly tense, thick with
an uncomfortable silence as Briseis and I locked eyes, both unsure
of how to proceed.

"So?" she spoke, her voice laced with a hint of petulance. "Talk."

I struggled to find the right words, my mind racing to make a
connection with this woman who seemed so guarded and resentful.
"I'm...Patroklos," I finally managed to say, my voice wavering with
uncertainty.

Her response was swift and cutting. "I don't care," she retorted,
dismissing my introduction with a cold indifference.

Frustration welled up within me, and I felt compelled to make her
understand. "I-I... I'm not your enemy!" I exclaimed, my voice tinged
with exasperation. "I want to help!"

Her eyes narrowed, her tone dripping with sarcasm. "And how will
you do that?" she challenged, her voice laced with bitterness. "Will
you release me and send me home safely? Will you also release all
of the other people you've taken captive? Will you leave my country
and let us be in peace? No? I didn't think so!" Her words were
filled with a mix of anger and despair, expressing the deep pain and
resentment she held towards our actions.

A fervent yearning surged within me, compelling me to earn her
trust. The inexplicable depth of this desire consumed my thoughts,
urging me to take action. In a surge of raw emotion, I unsheathed my
gleaming spear, its polished surface catching the glimmering light,
and with a swift, decisive motion, I sliced through the coarse rope
that bound her delicate hands to the bed.

Her countenance displayed a mixture of bewilderment and disbelief as she gingerly massaged the crimson imprints encircling her wrists.

"You must be either incredibly naive or foolish," she declared, her voice tinged with skepticism.

"Perhaps a bit of both," I quipped, attempting to lighten the mood. A subtle tilt of her lips betrayed a hint of a smile, a small but significant sign that she was gradually embracing my presence.

A heavy sigh escaped her lips, her demeanor softened slightly as she regarded me with a mix of curiosity and scepticism.

"So, what is it that you want?" she inquired, her voice laced with a hint of weariness.

"I want to help," I replied earnestly, my voice tinged with conviction. "I want to alleviate the suffering caused by this war, especially for your people. I've witnessed the atrocities committed by the Spartans against them, and it's not right."

"How do you plan on doing that?" she questioned, her eyes narrowing in suspicion.

"With your assistance," I responded, my voice unwavering. "I've offered aid in tending to their wounds, and I've even offered them food, but they refused my help."

A glimmer of frustration flickered in her eyes as she spoke, "My people are stubborn like that. They would rather die than accept aid from Greek scum."

I winced at the harshness of her words, feeling the weight of shame and embarrassment for the actions of my people.

"But you're not like them," she said, her voice carrying a mix of curiosity and intrigue. "You're...different. Weird, but different."

A genuine smile spread across my face, my eyes sparkling with excitement as she acknowledged my desire to assist her people.

"So, you'll help me then?" I asked, my voice filled with hope and anticipation.

"First," she began, her tone shifting to a more serious note. "I need to ensure the safety of my cousin, Chryseis, and then my Uncle."

"Alright," I responded, my mind racing with a plan. "The captives are nearby. I suggest we search for your uncle first, and then we can check on your cousin."

Briseis studied me for a moment, her gaze lingering as if contemplating her decision. Uncertainty clouded my thoughts, unsure if she would change her mind about assisting me. However, after a brief pause, she finally spoke.

"Fine, let's go," she declared, determination etching her voice. And so, with a shared purpose, we embarked towards the nearby jail pens.

The jail pens were grim, metallic enclosures that confined a pitiful gathering of captives. Squeezed together like sardines, the cages were only spacious enough to accommodate six or seven individuals, resulting in a desperate and cramped atmosphere.

The scorching sun bore down relentlessly upon the Trojan citizens, as there was no ceiling to shield them from its punishing rays. Their skin had become a fiery shade of red, their lips cracked and parched, and their bodies weakened by the harsh conditions.

My companion, Briseis, and I surveyed the scene with a mixture of horror and disbelief. The expression etched on her face spoke volumes, reflecting the profound anguish that had taken hold of her. This formidable woman, who had fearlessly confronted every danger so far, now teetered on the edge of tears

As Briseis made eye contact with some of the captive souls, their desperate pleas for assistance reached her ears. She engaged in conversation with them, offering solace and companionship in their dire circumstances, while also inquiring about the whereabouts of her uncle.

Amidst the sea of desperate faces, one man's voice pierced through the cacophony, drawing Briseis's attention. In a gesture of solidarity, she clasped his hand tightly, lending him a glimmer of hope in the midst of their shared despair.

"Briseis!" the man's voice cracked with relief and gratitude. "Thank the Gods you're safe."

Her voice trembled as she asked, her tone gentle yet filled with anguish, "Where is my uncle?"

A profound sorrow swept over the man's face, his eyes welling up with unshed tears. "He... he didn't survive the torture," he choked out, his voice heavy with grief. It was as if his tears had been exhausted, leaving him with a hollow shell of emotions.

For a moment, she stood there, frozen in place, as if struggling to process the enormity of her loss.

Before Briseis, and I could even begin to process the shocking news, a figure emerged in a hurry. It was Eurypylus, his breath labored as he sprinted towards us.

"Patroklos!" he gasped, his voice filled with urgency. "Lord Agamemnon is urgently summoning all troops to assemble at the shield!"

Briseis, her voice laced with authority, wasted no time in demanding information. "Is Chryseis with him?" she demanded, her tone brooking no argument. The forcefulness of her inquiry caused

Eurypylus to instinctively take a step back, his eyes widening in surprise.

Sensing the boy's unease, I offered a reassuring presence. "It's alright," I said, my voice calm and soothing. "You can answer her."

Reluctantly, the boy nodded in response, his apprehension palpable in the air.

Without a moment's hesitation, Briseis began striding towards the city gates, her movements purposeful and determined. Meanwhile, I placed a firm hand on Eurypylus' shoulder, my grip tight and unyielding.

"Stay here at camp," I instructed him, my tone brooking no argument. "If anything happens, seek refuge in the temple. Do you understand?"

The boy opened his mouth to protest, but I cut him off before he could utter a single word. "That's an order," I declared, my voice firm and commanding. With that, I turned on my heel and began walking briskly after Briseis, my steps quick and determined. I knew I couldn't afford to let her get too far ahead of me, not with all that emotion consuming her.

As the chaos of the soldiers engulfed us, Briseis vanished from sight. I frantically scanned the tumultuous scene, desperately hoping to catch a glimpse of her, but she was nowhere to be found.

My attention was drawn to the front, where Achilles stood, leading our Myrmidons. Behind him, the mass of soldiers surged forward, their determination palpable. In front of them, the two Kings stood with an air of authority. Agamemnon, holding Chryseis tightly in his arms, raised his voice, his words piercing through the clamor and reaching the heavens as I approached Achilles.

Confused and anxious, I turned to Achilles, seeking answers. "What's happening?" I implored, my voice tinged with worry.

Achilles sighed, his frustration evident in his grumble. "Hopefully nothing..." he muttered, his gaze fixed on the King. "...that shield is mine to take down."

Agamemnon's voice reverberated through the air, carrying his words to the heavens. "Apollo! Mighty sun God!" he bellowed, his voice commanding attention. "I hold your dear chosen priestess in my arms! I wish to give her to you in exchange for the city of Troy!"

The stillness of the surroundings was palpable, as if time had come to a standstill. Not a single sound could be heard, as if even the wind held its breath in anticipation.

Agamemnon's voice, now laced with impatience and frustration, pierced through the stillness, reverberating into the vast expanse. "Answer me, sun God!" he demanded, his words echoing off the surrounding walls.

Yet, the silence persisted, unyielding and unbroken. The absence of any divine intervention left us suspended in a state of uncertainty, our hearts pounding with trepidation. Would the mighty Apollo heed Agamemnon's plea, or would he remain aloof to the mortal king's entreaties?

Agamemnon's frustration boiled over, his voice rising to a thunderous roar. "Fine!" he bellowed, his anger palpable. "I have shown you honor, but you have chosen to ignore me! If the gods will not intervene, then as her master, I shall assert my dominance over her!"

In the midst of the lingering silence, a sudden disruption shattered the stillness. The piercing caw of a crow sliced through the air, its shrill cry reverberating through the surrounding landscape.

We instinctively turned our heads, scanning the horizon in search of the source of this unexpected intrusion. And then, against the backdrop of the sun's radiant glow, a small silhouette emerged, gradually growing larger as it drew nearer.

As the bird approached, its presence became more imposing, its cawing growing louder with each passing moment. The sound resonated through the land, echoing off the hills and valleys, as if the very earth itself was responding to the crow's call.

The crow, a creature of immense proportions, soared above us, its colossal wingspan erupting flames that caused us all to instinctively duck in response. Its feathers, as pale as freshly fallen snow, stood out against the vibrant sky, a stark contrast to its dark, beady eyes that seemed to hold a mysterious wisdom. I couldn't help but wonder if this was the same enigmatic crow that I had once glimpsed perched atop the temple window, its presence imbued with an otherworldly aura.

As the crow descended, its wings beating with a rhythmic grace, a dazzling transformation unfolded before our eyes. In a burst of radiant sparks, the bird dissolved into nothingness, leaving in its wake the ethereal form of a God.

Before us stood a figure of unparalleled beauty, his divine presence illuminating the surrounding landscape. His skin, kissed by the sun's golden rays, glowed with a celestial radiance, while his hair shimmered like strands of flaming gold. Every feature of his face was sculpted with perfection, exuding an ageless youthfulness that seemed to defy mortal limitations.

But it was his eyes that held me captive, their brilliance piercing through the very depths of my soul. They gleamed with an otherworldly luminescence, a radiant white that seemed to emanate a power beyond mortal comprehension. In their depths, one could glimpse the wisdom of ages, the secrets of the universe, and the boundless authority of a God.

We stood there, awestruck and humbled, as the divine presence took hold of our senses. Agamemnon, the mighty king, stood frozen in place, his mouth agape, unable to utter a single word in the face of such divine magnificence.

The God approached him with an air of superiority, his every step resonating with an earth-shaking force that seemed to command the very ground beneath him. As he drew nearer, his presence grew in intensity, emanating an aura of authority that enveloped the mortal king in a suffocating grip.

His voice, a deep and resonant rumble, reverberated through the air, carrying with it a sense of both menace and command. "You are nothing but mere bones," he growled, his words laced with a divine power that sent tremors through Agamemnon's very being. "I could scorch you with just one glance, and yet you dare humiliate me."

Agamemnon, once a proud and boastful king, now found himself reduced to a mere puppet in the presence of the divine. His voice, once filled with arrogance and bravado, was now reduced to a mere whisper, barely audible in the face of such overwhelming authority. He stood there, his mouth agape, his body frozen in place, as the weight of the God's words bore down upon him.

"This woman, and this city, is under my protection," the God continued, his voice carrying an unyielding conviction. "So don't dare threaten me again, mortal, or I'll make it your last breath."

Apollo stretched his arm towards Chryseis, his palm open, awaiting for hers to hold his. With a smile from the radiant God, a beam of light surrounded them, blinding in its brilliance. In an instant, they disappeared, leaving Agamemnon standing alone, his heart heavy with regret and the realization of his own insignificance in the face of divine power

As the chaos unfolded before me, Briseis, fueled by a burning rage, charged towards Agamemnon with a stolen soldier's sword clutched tightly in her hands. Her eyes blazed with a fierce determination as she sought to exact her revenge upon the man who had taken everything from her.

With an animalistic scream, she lunged at Agamemnon, her sword poised to strike. But before she could reach him, King Menelaus, swift and decisive, intercepted her attack. With a powerful blow to her face, Briseis crumpled to the ground, her body wracked with pain. Two soldiers swiftly pinned her down, their grip unyielding.

Menelaus winced, a grimace of pain etched upon his face as blood trickled down his arm from the cut inflicted by Briseis. Despite the injury, he managed to muster a dry quip, his voice laced with a mix of annoyance and resignation. "Ugh...Great. Another scar to add to the collection."

Agamemnon, finally regaining his voice after his encounter with Apollo, sneered at Briseis, his anger seething through his words. "You dare attack me, slave!? I am your master!" His hand rose, ready to deliver a punishing blow, but before it could descend, Achilles, swift and protective, seized Agamemnon's hand, halting its trajectory mid-thrust.

"I am her master," Achilles declared, his voice filled with a quiet intensity. "You do not have permission to touch my slave."

The look on Agamemnon's face was a twisted mask of fury, his eyes burning with a mixture of rage and annoyance.

Agamemnon's face contorted with rage as he bellowed, his voice laced with a mix of fury and desperation. "She nearly brought about my demise! I implore you, as recompense for your failure to control her, return her to my possession!" Agamemnon's eyes burned with accusation, his words dripping with disdain for the Prince. "Your incompetence has left me questioning your value, Prince. Thus far, your contributions have amounted to nothing more than a few feeble sparks and a lackluster display of airborne prowess. I find myself doubting if you are truly deserving of being your father's son."

"You dare mock me, King?" The intensity in his voice was palpable, a reflection of the smoldering rage surging within him.

Agamemnon smirked, his eyes narrowing with a hint of malicious amusement. "Surely, I cannot be mistaken in my assessment, can I? Unless, of course, you possess the ability to present evidence to the contrary?" His taunting tone hung in the air, a challenge laced with arrogance.

Achilles stood tall, his voice steady and resolute, as he shot back with unwavering confidence. "You are wrong." Achilles stated confidently.

Agamemnon's face twisted with a mix of frustration and disbelief, his voice laced with a demanding tone. "Then prove it! Remove that shield this instant!"

Achilles, undeterred by Agamemnon's challenge, stood with unwavering resolve. His eyes locked onto Agamemnon's, a fierce determination burning within them. With a steady voice, he issued his defiant response. "No."

Agamemnon's brows furrowed in a mixture of astonishment and confusion, his voice betraying his disbelief. "What did you just say?"

The words tumbled out, a mix of incredulity and uncertainty, as he struggled to comprehend Achilles' refusal.

"You insulted me. You can keep the airships and my troops as your pact with my father still stands. You can also have the girl as an apology, but I refuse to fight for you any longer."

My voice caught in my throat as I called out to Achilles, a sense of surprise and disbelief coursing through me. How could he simply give up Briseis? And what about the shield, the very purpose for us both being here? Was could he abandon that too just like that?

Achilles spun around sharply, his expression unreadable, as he began to stride away, heedless of my calls for him.

Chapter 18

<hr>

"Why would you let him take her?!" I yelled at Achilles in frustration, my voice piercing through the stillness of the night. The moon bathed our tent in a soft glow, casting long shadows on the ground.

Within the confined space, Eurypylus stood silently in the corner, his presence a mere shadow in the dim light.

"She tried to kill him and she wounded Menelaus," Achilles responded casually, his voice calm and collected. "I had to give her to him as recompense."

"And what about the shield? Are you just giving up after everything we've been through?" I asked, bewildered by the sudden shift in his purpose for being here.

Achilles scoffed at my question, his gaze filled with determination. "Don't be ridiculous. I will bring down that shield, but I will not stand for Agamemnon's insults. I am his plan, his key to victory. Without me, he has nothing. He knows this, and soon he will come begging. Then, and only then, I will take down the barrier. That way, I keep my respect, my honor, and I reclaim my glory."

"And what about Briseis? Will you demand her return?" I asked, my voice filled with concern.

"If that is your wish, then I will make the demand. But do not expect Agamemnon to comply," Achilles replied, his tone laced with skepticism.

"There must be a way to persuade him-" I insisted, hoping for a resolution.

Achilles interrupted me, his eyes filled with a mix of irritation and curiosity. "Why do you care so much about her? You've only just met her today," he questioned.

I paused, searching for the right words to express my feelings. "She is a victim of this war. She deserves our help, my help," I said firmly, my conviction unwavering. "I cannot stand by and watch her suffer."

Achilles looked at me, his gaze piercing. "Are you certain this is what you truly want? Does she even desire your assistance? Is she even worth the trouble?"

Without hesitation, I affirmed, "Yes. She is worth it. I want to bring her solace and aid in any way I can. While you seek glory through war, I aspire to find mine through benevolence."

Achilles sighed, recognizing the determination in my eyes. "Very well. I will ensure that Agamemnon returns her to us, but not before he apologizes to me for his insolence."

"Thank you," I beamed, my arms instinctively wrapping around his strong frame. Achilles reciprocated the embrace, holding me close. We stood there, entwined, finding solace in each other's presence. The weight of the world fading away momentarily.

"Should I leave you two alone?" the young boy asked, his voice laced with awkwardness.

We turned to him, realizing we had forgotten his presence. "You can have the temple all to yourself tonight," I said sweetly, offering him a small smile. Eurypylus returned the smile and exited the tent, leaving Achilles and me alone.

"It's been a while since it was just the two of us." Achilles remarked, his hand holding mine.

I settled on his lap, feeling the familiar comfort of his touch. "There's only so much privacy you can get in a war camp, surrounded by hundreds of soldiers."

Achilles' touch traced a slow, deliberate path across my body, his fingers exploring every curve and contour, as if mapping the depths of my soul. The anticipation of my reaction lingered in the air, a palpable energy that crackled between us.

Unable to resist the pull any longer, I leaned in and our lips met, a magnetic force drawing us together. In that instant, the desire to connect with him consumed me, overpowering any thought or worry that might have lingered in my mind.

It had been far too long since we had simply sat together in silence, basking in the warmth of each other's presence. As the passion enveloped us, my hands roamed his body, mirroring the fervor that coursed through my veins. Our breaths quickened, becoming erratic as the urge to make love grew overwhelming.

With a strength that belied his warrior's frame, Achilles effortlessly lifted me and laid me gently upon his bed. In the blink of an eye, our clothes were discarded, scattered across the room like remnants of a battle fought and won. Our lips found each other once again, a fervent dance of desire and longing.

The rhythm of Achilles' body melded seamlessly with mine, and together we moaned in a frenzy of raw emotion. I felt the force of his hips thrust against me, each movement sending waves of euphoria crashing through my senses. Overwhelmed by the pleasure, I clutched onto his hair, anchoring myself to the moment.

"Achilles!" I cried out, my voice a symphony of ecstasy as he responded with an intensified rhythm, driving us both to the brink of release.

The bliss became almost unbearable, a crescendo of sensation that engulfed us both until we reached the pinnacle of our passion in a climactic finale. Our bodies trembling and convulsing from from our dance of love.

We lay still on his bed, the memories of our shared life flooding my mind. I remembered the first time I laid eyes on him, the first time we swam together, the first time we argued and fought, and the first time our skins touched. I chuckled at the thought of those moments.

"What is it?" he asked, his voice filled with curiosity.

"Just reminiscing," I replied, unable to contain my smile. I turned my head to the side and saw his eyes gazing at me. In moments like this, where nothing else mattered but him and me, his eyes resembled the vast ocean, full of uncharted wonders.

"I love you," I blurted out, unable to hold it in any longer. His eyes widened in surprise, but a smile slowly spread across his face.

"I love you too," he replied, and our lips met once again, sealing our love in that tender moment of respite.

Chapter 19

As the weight of exhaustion settled upon me, my vision gradually dimmed, signaling the imminent arrival of sleep. However, just as I was about to succumb to its embrace, a cacophony of footsteps echoed outside our tent, resonating with such force that it seemed as if the very ground beneath us trembled.

Startled from our drowsy state, both Achilles and I hastily donned our tunics, our senses now heightened with a mix of curiosity and apprehension. With a sense of urgency, Achilles confronted the intruder, his voice laced with authority and a demand for answers.

"Who are you?!" Achilles demanded, his eyes narrowing as he sought to unveil the identity of the trespasser.

"Apologies for the intrusion," the man spoke, his voice carrying a weight that demanded attention. He cleared his throat, as if to gather his thoughts before continuing. "I had hoped for a more favorable setting in which to meet you both," he said, his gaze shifting between me and Achilles. "However, the matter at hand is of utmost importance, especially for you, child of Thetis."

Achilles and I exchanged glances, a mixture of surprise and reverence etching itself onto our faces. It dawned on us that the divine presence standing before us was none other than the God of the ocean himself. In an instant, Achilles instinctively bowed, his body bending in deference to the deity. I followed suit, my movements mirroring his in a show of respect.

The god's hair, dark and damp, seemed as if it had endured years submerged beneath the depths of the sea. His eyes, unlike the vibrant hues of Apollo, possessed a deep blue reminiscent of the unfathomable abyss that lay hidden within the ocean's depths.

"Stand up child," Poseidon commanded, his voice resonating with a mixture of paternal warmth and authority. "I've know your mother for years. no need for formalities."

"Thank you, mighty sea God," Achilles uttered, his voice tinged with reverence. "Pray, enlighten us on the purpose of your visit. What is it that you have come to discuss?"

"Not a mere discussion, but a grave warning," the sea God began, his voice carrying the weight of ancient wisdom. "We, Gods, have long adhered to an agreement, one that forbids our direct interference in the conflicts of mortals. However, when Apollo descended from the heavens and abducted his priestess, he breached this sacred pact, opening the floodgates for all of us to intervene in this war. And my family shall intervene, for they are not the type to miss such an opportunity."

Poseidon's words hung in the air, heavy with the foreboding of impending turmoil. His hand, adorned with markings that resembled swirling waves, rested upon Achilles' shoulder, the touch both comforting and ominous. I couldn't help but trace my gaze along the intricate patterns that encircled the god's arm, their fluidity mirroring the ebb and flow of the ocean's currents.

"I understand your unwavering determination to partake in this war," Poseidon continued, his voice tinged with a mixture of sympathy and caution. "Therefore, I shall impart upon you the knowledge of how to breach that impenetrable shield."

Achilles and I exchanged glances, our attention fully captured by the god's words. Anticipation coursed through our veins as we awaited the revelation that would shape the course of our destiny.

"The shield...Apollo created it," Poseidon's voice resonated with a mixture of anger and disappointment. His eyes, once filled with warmth, now held a glint of resentment as he recounted the events that led to the shield's creation. "Both of us sought to be patrons of Troy, but Apollo seized the city for himself. The Trojans, swayed by his ability to shield them from the scorching sun, chose him as their patron."

The god's words hung in the air, heavy with the weight of ancient grudges. He continued, his voice carrying a sense of determination. "The shield draws its power from the sun, but fear not, for I possess the ability to temporarily shut it down. My control over the sky may not match that of my brother's, but it will grant you enough time to infiltrate and dismantle it from within. Do keep in mind, that you only have one chance at this."

With a graceful movement, Poseidon extended his hand towards Achilles, offering him a whistle in the shape of a majestic horse. The intricate details of the whistle revealed the god's craftsmanship, each curve and line resembling the strength and power of the creature it represented.

Silently, Poseidon turned and left the tent, his departure marked by the absence of further words. Achilles and I exchanged glances, the weight of the task ahead settling upon us. The whistle, now cradled in Achilles' hand, held the key to ending the war that had consumed our lives. It was a symbol of hope and a reminder that our actions would determine the fate of countless lives.

Achilles held the horse-shaped whistle in his hands, his eyes fixated upon it with a mixture of awe and uncertainty

As I spoke, excitement and hope filled my voice, my words echoing through the tent. "This means we can win. If we do this right, you might not die after all!"

I couldn't contain my joy, my arms wrapping tightly around Achilles in an embrace of triumph. The weight of the war seemed to lift from our shoulders, replaced by a renewed sense of purpose and determination. But as I held him, I felt a strange absence in his response, a lack of reciprocation in his embrace

Pulling away, I gazed into Achilles' eyes, searching for the source of his sudden change in demeanor. His face, once filled with happiness, now appeared blank, his expression distant and troubled. Concern washed over me as I reached out to touch his arm gently.

"What's wrong, Achilles?" I asked, my voice laced with genuine concern as I peered into his troubled eyes.

"This doesn't feel right," he murmured, his voice tinged with a mix of disappointment and unease. "It feels cheap...a hollow victory."

I blinked in disbelief, my mind struggling to comprehend his words. "But Achilles," I stammered, trying to make sense of his perspective, "you heard Poseidon himself. The other Gods will surely intervene. We can not afford to squander this opportunity. "

Achilles shook his head, his expression resolute. "I understand the stakes, but I already have the aid of a God," he said, his voice filled with arrogance. "This spear is a weapon strong enough to crack the sky open if I want it to, I don't need Poseidon's help as well."

Frustration surged through me, fueling my words as I confronted Achilles. "So, let me get this straight," I seethed, my voice laced with anger and disbelief. "You're seriously going to keep trying to break through the shield with that spear, even though it's failed every time thus far?"

Achilles met my fiery gaze with an air of composed determination, his voice steady and resolute. "No," he replied, his tone betraying a cool resolve. "I've made myself clear. I refuse to take any action until Agamemnon offers a genuine apology, acknowledging the deep offence he has caused me. Only then will I even consider using the power of the whistle."

His words hung in the air, a tense silence enveloping us as the weight of his decision settled upon my shoulders. I couldn't believe that the fate of so many lives rested on the shoulders of a prideful King and an arrogant Prince.

My voice trembled with a mix of desperation and frustration as I confronted Achilles, my words echoing through the tense atmosphere. "The Gods will inevitably intervene, Achilles! Are you truly willing to wait until Agamemnon humbles himself and offers an apology before taking action? What about the countless soldiers who will perish in the meantime? What about our brothers, whose lives hang in the balance?"

Achilles' expression remained stoic, his resolve unyielding as he delivered his response. "If the Gods are foolish enough to unleash their wrath upon my soldiers, then I will intervene," he declared, his voice carrying an air of unwavering determination. "But as long as they remain unharmed, I will not be swayed."

My heart sank at his words, the weight of the impending danger pressing upon me. I knew that time was of the essence, that every moment wasted in this standoff risked the lives of countless warriors. A surge of determination coursed through my veins as I made up my mind.

"Then I will go warn them." I declared abruptly, my voice tinged with urgency.

Achilles merely nodded, his gaze fixed on some distant point beyond the confines of the tent. "Go ahead," he replied, his tone devoid of resistance. "I won't stop you."

Without another word, I hurriedly exited the tent, my mind racing with a mix of determination and apprehension

As I hurried through the bustling camp, the air thick with the scent of sweat and anticipation, I couldn't help but notice the jovial atmosphere that seemed to permeate the soldiers' conversations. Laughter echoed through the air, mingling with the clinking of cups and the savoury aromas of roasted meat. But amidst the mirth, a chilling scream pierced the tranquillity, causing my heart to lurch in my chest.

I turned, my eyes widening in horror as I witnessed a Spartan soldier collapse in agony, his body writhing uncontrollably on the ground. With a surge of adrenaline, I rushed to his side, my hands trembling as I tried to ease his suffering. But as I pried his fingers away from his face, a sight of pure horror awaited me.

His once handsome features were now marred by a grotesque red rash, his skin bubbling and oozing with a sickening fluid. His eyes, once full of life, were now hidden beneath the ravages of the infection. A wave of despair washed over me as I realized that this was not an isolated incident.

The screams multiplied, a cacophony of pain and terror that reverberated through the camp. I could no longer ignore the urgency of the situation. Every passing moment meant more lives lost to this mysterious affliction. Determination fueled my steps as I sprinted towards Agamemnon's tent, the image of the suffering soldiers etched into my mind.

As I burst into the tent, my breath came in ragged gasps, my eyes darting around the space. There, in the dimly lit corner, lay Briseis, bound and helpless. My heart clenched at the sight, but I forced myself to focus on the matter at hand. Agamemnon stood before me, his posture exuding arrogance and indifference, flanked by his brother and two soldiers.

The soldiers, their expressions, a mix of confusion and concern, formed a barrier between me and Agamemnon. Their hands gripped their weapons tightly, ready to defend their leader at a moment's notice. Agamemnon's eyes bore into mine, demanding answers, his voice laced with impatience.

"What is going on out there?" he bellowed, his voice reverberating through the tent. "Speak, boy!"

But before I could utter a word, Menelaus, Agamemnon's brother, intervened. His voice, though firm, carried a hint of understanding. "Let him go," he commanded, his tone brooking no argument. The guard released his grip on me, allowing me to step forward and face the two brothers.

Taking a deep breath, I began to recount the events that had unfolded before my eyes. I described the soldiers' writhing in agony, their bodies consumed by a mysterious infection. I explained how the Gods, in their wrath, had decided to intervene in the war, and how Achilles had issued his demand for an apology as a condition for victory.

"You must be jesting!" Agamemnon scoffed, his voice dripping with arrogance. His words hung in the air, heavy with disdain. "I will not apologize to him! If the Gods are getting involved, then that must mean that we also will have assistance from them! You can tell that little brat that we will not be requiring his incompetence any longer."

His words struck me like a physical blow, the weight of his stubbornness crashing down upon me. I felt a mix of anger and desperation welling up inside me, threatening to spill over. But before I could respond, Agamemnon waved his hand dismissively, signaling the soldiers to escort me out of the tent.

As I stepped outside, a scene of devastation unfolded before me. The once bustling camp was now littered with bodies, soldiers writhing in pain and agony. Their faces contorted in anguish, their bodies twisted and contorted by the mysterious infection

My heart sank as I realized the magnitude of the crisis. The lives of our comrades hung in the balance, and Agamemnon's stubbornness threatened to condemn them to a gruesome fate.

Chapter 20

As the first rays of morning light pierced through the somber sky, a suffocating atmosphere of darkness and despair still engulfed the scene before my eyes. The sheer magnitude of lifeless bodies that we had to burn, weighed heavily on my soul, each one a haunting testament to the mercilessness of Apollo's wrath.

Desperate for solace and guidance, I turned my gaze heavenward, beseeching the divine forces that governed our fates. With fervent devotion, I directed my entreaties to every deity imaginable, hoping that even one would heed my plea and offer respite from this grim reality. Yet, the heavens remained silent, their celestial inhabitants seemingly indifferent to the suffering below.

Amidst the chaos, a chorus of voices rose, imploring, Agamemnon, to seek absolution from Apollo. The weight of guilt and regret hung heavy in the air, as many believed that appeasing the wrathful deity was the key to ending this unnecessary bloodshed. However, the stubborn resolve of the King remained unyielding, unswayed by the desperate pleas of his subjects.

The sickness had momentarily released its hold, but the lingering fear of its return or the emergence of an even greater affliction weighed heavily on my mind. The sleepless night had been filled with anxiety and restlessness, and so seeking refuge, I made my way towards the sacred temple, hoping to find a moment of tranquility within its hallowed walls. However, just as I approached the entrance, a deafening explosion shattered the air, its thunderous reverberations jolting me from my thoughts.

In an instant, the calm atmosphere was shattered, replaced by a frantic flurry of activity. Soldiers scrambled to arm themselves, hastily grabbing their weapons and donning their armor, their faces etched with a mixture of determination and trepidation. Amidst the chaos, I caught sight of the two kings as they emerged from their tent in a rush.

Driven by a sense of urgency and curiosity, I hurried towards them, my footsteps echoing in the tense atmosphere. As I approached Menelaus, his expression betraying a mixture of concern and resolve, I mustered the courage to inquire about the cause of the commotion, desperately seeking answers in the midst of uncertainty.

"The airships have been destroyed! The Trojans are launching an attack!" Menelaus' voice reverberated with urgency, carrying the weight of the devastating news.

"Destroyed?! How?!" I questioned as my voice shook and heart skipped a beat with disbelief and confusion. How could such marvels of technology, seemingly impervious to destruction, meet such a fate? The Trojans, formidable as they were, lacked the means to accomplish such a feat.

"It had to be Apollo. We've angered him and you haven't made this situation any better by refusing to apologise to him!" Menelaus declared, his voice tinged with accusation as he turned his gaze towards Agamemnon. The tension between the two kings hung palpably in the air, their disagreement a reflection of the tumultuous times we found ourselves in

Agamemnon's face hardened, his resolve unyielding as he vehemently defended his stance. "I will not bow to a God who sides with those barbarians! Do not fret brother, we will win this war! We also have deities on our side, I can feel their presence."

As everyone readied themselves for battle, I could see the Trojans riding towards us with a ferocity and determination that sent a chill down my spine.

Suddenly,a voice pierced through the clamor, calling my name with a sense of urgency. I turned, my heart pounding in my chest, to see a fellow Myrmidon soldier approaching me. His face bore a mix of concern and urgency, as he delivered the news that sent a wave of panic crashing over me.

"Lord Patroklos! You must come to the infirmary. A young soldier is calling for you."

In that moment, time seemed to stand still as the weight of my forgotten duty bore down on me like an oppressive weight.

Without a moment's hesitation, my body moved on its own accord, propelled by a surge of adrenaline and a desperate need to rectify my neglect. The chaos around me faded into the background as I sprinted towards the infirmary, my mind consumed with guilt and worry. How could I have forgotten about Eurypylus? I had been so preoccupied with assisting others that I had forgotten to check up on him.

I reached the infirmary and saw several soldiers on the verge of death. Although the infection hadn't claimed them yet, their fate was inevitable. Even our potent ambrosia potions couldn't act swiftly enough to save them.

My eyes darted desperately from one bed to another, my heart pounding in my chest as I searched for Eurypylus amidst the sea of suffering. Finally, I spotted Eurypylus, his once vibrant figure reduced to a mere shell of his former self. The infection had taken hold across his face and body, transforming him into a grotesque figure. My heart shattered at the sight, a mixture of guilt and sorrow washing over me like a tidal wave.

Falling to my knees by his side, I clutched his hand in mine, the touch offering a fleeting connection amidst the chaos. His effort to speak was met with a harsh cough, his lips tainted with blood, which I tenderly wiped away from his mouth with my garment.

As my hands trembled with a mixture of fear and desperation, I became acutely aware of the dry blood that coated my skin. The crimson stains stood out starkly against the pale backdrop of the infirmary, a gruesome reminder of the horrors that surrounded us. It was a chilling realization, the fact that I had been immersed in this sea of blood and suffering without even noticing.

"Don't speak, Eurypylus," I pleaded, my voice choked with emotion. I held onto his hand with a grip so tight that my own fingers grew numb, as if trying to anchor him to this world. But his attempts to communicate were met with wheezing and violent coughs, each expulsion of breath accompanied by a spray of blood. It was a horrifying sight, a visceral reminder of the infection's relentless grip on his frail body.

In one swift, heart-wrenching moment, Eurypylus' hand slipped from mine. I shook him, my voice filled with desperation as I called out his name, but it was futile. The boy who had once been full of life had succumbed to the infection, releasing his soul into Thanatos' chilling embrace. The weight of his loss settled heavily on my shoulders, a burden I could not bear.

I looked around the infirmary, the scene of tragedy unfolding before me. The air was heavy with the stench of death and despair, the groans of the wounded mixing with the anguished cries of those on the brink of their final breath. It was a sight that tore at my soul.

In that moment, a fire ignited within me, fueled by a determination to make a difference. If Achilles, consumed by his own ego, would not step up to help these wounded soldiers, then I would be the one to do it. I would not let their sacrifices be in vain.

Chapter 21

The clash between the Spartans and the Trojans was like a collision of two mighty waves, each crashing against the other with a force that sent blood soaring from their bodies. The battlefield reverberated with the sound of clashing weapons, the metallic echoes filling the air. Above, airships soared to provide aid, but their valiant efforts were swiftly crushed as a golden projectile pierced through their defenses, reducing them to mere dust in an instant.

I entered our tent as the cries of wounded soldiers echoed outside. Inside, Achilles sat upon his chair, the same spot where I had left him before, but now he was engaged in a different pursuit. His fingers danced upon the strings of his lyre, producing a melody that seemed to drown out the cries from outside. And he sang...

"Oh, stand with me," he sang, his voice filled with a raw vulnerability, "through the trials we face, In this realm of wonder, our hearts embrace..." In that fleeting moment, as his voice enveloped the space around us, I caught a glimpse of a different man. The man I had fallen in love with, the man I yearned for him to remain.

"Achilles!" I called out to him, my voice cutting through the air and shattering the fragile tranquility that had enveloped the tent. He turned his head towards me, his piercing blue eyes locking onto mine, a mix of surprise and curiosity etched across his face.

"You already know," he began, his voice carrying a hint of resignation, "that I won't fight. Agamemnon has made his choice."

"I know," I responded, my voice filled with determination, "That's why I'll be the one to do it!"

My declaration hung heavily in the air, and I watched as his expression transformed from surprise to sheer shock. His usually composed face now contorted with disbelief, his lips parted as if trying to form words that simply refused to escape.

"Wh--You--" he stammered, his voice trembling with a vulnerability I had never witnessed before. For once in his life, Achilles, the mighty warrior, was at a loss for words. It was evident that he had no idea how to respond to my unwavering statement.

"You refuse to fight because of your ego," I began, my voice carrying an undercurrent of frustration and disappointment. "You are willing to let countless lives be lost, all while clinging to the title of a hero. But true heroism isn't about dying in a grand battle; it's about sacrificing yourself in the most brutal way imaginable for the sake of others. If your pride blinds you to this truth and prevents you from taking action, then let me take your place!"

Achilles looked at me, his eyes filled with a mixture of confusion and disbelief. His brow arched in an attempt to comprehend my words. "Take my place?" he questioned, his voice tinged with confusion.

"Yes," I affirmed, my voice unwavering. "Give me your armor, your spear. I will pretend to be you. If the Spartans see me and believe you are fighting alongside them, perhaps we stand a chance at victory. I can move like you, fight like you, speak like you. So let me pretend I'm you."

As my words settled in the air, his reaction was immediate and intense. He lunged forward, gripping my shoulders with a sudden rush of emotion. His eyes bore into mine, filled with a mixture of concern and desperation. "Pretend!" he exclaimed, his voice trembling with a raw intensity. "All you can do is pretend! You aren't me! You will die!"

His words stung, but I refused to let doubt cloud my determination. "We have both undergone the same training, honed the same skills." I argued, my voice steady.

"But you've never killed anyone! And I know that you never will. So when that moment comes where you have to take a life...you won't." He confessed, his voice tinged with a mix of sadness and certainty.

I met his gaze, unwavering despite the tremors of uncertainty that threatened to shake me. "I don't need to kill anyone. I'll just inspire them, instill hope within their hearts. I will show them that you are there, fighting alongside them. They have all witnessed the devastating power of your weapon. The Trojans will cower and flee as soon as they lay eyes on me."

Achilles stared into my eyes, his gaze unyielding. He understood the gravity of the situation, torn between his desire to protect me and the realization that my resolve was unyielding. He knew that if he refused, I would venture out into the battlefield alone, without his armor or spear, and face certain death.

"Just...Just promise me," his voice quivered, betraying the cracks in his composure, "promise me that you will drive the Trojans back to the shield, and then, without hesitation, return to my side." His words were fragile, as if they might shatter into a million pieces at any moment, but his unwavering gaze remained fixed on me.

"I'll be back." I replied, attempting to infuse my words with warmth and reassurance. But his face remained unchanged, etched with doubt and uncertainty.

"Why don't I believe you?" He questioned, his words hanging in the air like a haunting echo. I couldn't help but wonder if his doubt was directed at me, or himself.

As tears streamed down his face, I felt a surge of determination. I swiftly removed the bracelet from my wrist and pressed it into his trembling hand.

"I'll be back!" I declared, my voice now resolute and unwavering, as I locked eyes with him. "For this and for you." I promised.

I extended my hand, my touch gentle as I cradled the back of his head, my fingers gliding through the silky strands of his hair. Our lips met in a passionate, bittersweet embrace, a dance of longing and affection. As I reluctantly pulled away, I knew deep down that I had to be the one to do so, for if I didn't take this step, he would never let me go.

But before I could walk away, Achilles abruptly seized my arm and pressed my head against his own. With his eyes tightly closed, his breathing became more labored, and tears streamed down his cheeks.

In response, I closed my own eyes, allowing myself to be enveloped in our intimate moment. Time seemed to stand still as we held each other and we both found solace in the presence of one another. The world around us faded away, leaving only the two of us, connected in this delicate embrace.

The Myrmidons stood steadfastly by my side as I fearlessly led them towards the gruesome and chaotic battlefield. The air was thick with the metallic scent of blood, and the deafening sounds of clashing weapons and agonized screams filled the air.

My heart sank as I witnessed the horrifying scene unfolding before my eyes. Heads and limbs were mercilessly severed from the bodies of both friend and foe, painting the ground with a macabre canvas of crimson. It was enough to send shivers down my spine and make my stomach turn.

Amidst the chaos, countless soldiers, driven by a frenzied desire to defeat me, lunged forward in a desperate attempt to strike me down. Yet, with each encounter, I found myself skillfully incapacitating them, rendering them unconscious rather than delivering a fatal blow. Achilles' words echoed in my mind; he was right after all, I was incapable of taking another life.

As I continued to navigate through the battlefield, my actions did not go unnoticed by some of the Myrmidons. With unwavering loyalty and a sense of duty, they swiftly came to my aid, swiftly dispatching the soldiers who remained in my wake, ensuring that no lives were left behind.

When I had stepped onto the battlefield, a sense of despair hung heavy in the air, weighing down the spirits of the weary Spartans. Their once resolute faces wore expressions of defeat and resignation. However, as soon as they caught sight of me fighting alongside them, a flicker of hope ignited in their eyes, and they began fighting back relentlessly.

The scene that unfolded before me was nothing short of a nightmare. It was heart-wrenching to witness the sheer brutality and carnage that surrounded me. Each life lost felt like a blow to my own soul. Yet, even in the face of such devastation, I knew I could not falter. I had a duty to press forward, to fight for a cause greater than myself.

With grim determination, I pushed aside the overwhelming sorrow threatening to consume me. I drew strength from the unwavering resolve of my comrades, their unyielding spirit fueling my own. Together, we forged ahead, our collective will serving as a beacon of hope amidst the darkness of war.

As the chaos of the battlefield raged on, my eyes caught sight of a majestic horse galloping amidst the mayhem. Without hesitation, a surge of instinct propelled me to mount the steed, granting me a vantage point from which I could survey the unfolding battle. From this elevated position, I could witness the ebb and flow of the conflict with greater clarity.

The Trojans, though still fiercely engaged in combat, were gradually being pushed back towards the protective wall of their city. Their once formidable resistance now seemed to waver under the relentless assault of the Spartan forces.

Yet, amidst the cacophony of clashing weapons and desperate cries, a thunderous explosion erupted, shattering the air and sending shockwaves through the battlefield. The deafening blast annihilated a multitude of Spartan troops in an instant, leaving behind a scene of devastation.

As the dust settled, revealing a haze of particles hanging in the air, a figure emerged from the heart of the impact area. His presence was ominous, his eyes glowing a sinister shade of red that pierced through the gloom. In his hands, he wielded two axes, their gleaming blades glinting with a deadly purpose.

Dressed in a suit of dark armor, untouched by the chaos around him, he stood as a lone figure amidst the carnage. The design of his armor was simple yet striking, exuding an aura of power and intimidation. But it was his helmet that truly sent shivers down the spines of those who beheld it. It bore a terrifying visage, evoking fear and dread in all who gazed upon it. And beneath that menacing helmet, a smile that spoke volume of his intentions.

With a swift and practiced motion, he flung his axes through the air, the blades slicing through the bodies of countless soldiers with terrifying ease. Heads rolled, blood sprayed, and the once formidable warriors were reduced to lifeless corpses in an instant.

As if guided by an unseen force, the axes returned to their master, landing with a satisfying thud in his waiting hands. He surveyed the battlefield, a smug smirk playing upon his lips, reveling in the chaos and destruction he had wrought.

"Face me, sister!" His commanding voice reverberated across the battlefield, drowning out the clamor of clashing weapons. "Or I shall unleash further havoc upon your precious Greeks!"

The God's eyes blazed with a fiery determination as he poised himself to hurl his axes once more, his muscles taut with anticipation. But before he could release his deadly weapons, a resounding voice cut through the air like a thunderclap.

"Enough!" The woman's voice echoed with authority, carrying a weight that silenced even the most fervent of warriors. And then, from the heavens above, a magnificent owl descended, its wings outstretched. In the blink of an eye, the owl transformed into a majestic Goddess.

Radiating an aura of power and grace, the Goddess donned a golden helmet adorned with a blood-red plume, a striking symbol of her divine status. Her hair, dark and cascading, provided a stark contrast against the gleaming metal of her headpiece and her ethereal skin. In her hand, she held a gleaming spear, its point glinting with lethal intent. And in her other hand, she brandished a magnificent golden shield, its surface adorned with the visage of a woman and encircled by a multitude of intertwining snakes.

The clash of the Gods ignited a fierce battle that shook the very foundations of the land. Their divine powers clashed, causing shockwaves to ripple through the earth, as if the very ground itself trembled in awe of their might.

As I stood there, my gaze fixated on the distant walls of Troy, a sense of urgency and frustration welled up within me. My carefully crafted plan, my ruse of impersonating Achilles, had failed to yield the desired outcome. The Trojans remained resolute, refusing to surrender in the face of our relentless assault.

The chaos of battle surrounded me, the clash of weapons and the cries of warriors filling the air. In this moment, the city stood defenseless, vulnerable to my impending attack. There was no one to impede my progress, no force capable of halting my advance. The shield that protected Troy, a symbol of their resilience, beckoned to me, enticing me with the promise of victory.

With unwavering determination, I spurred my horse forward, its hooves thundering against the earth. Every beat of its powerful stride echoed my resolve, propelling me closer to my goal. Clutched tightly in my hand was the whistle I had taken from Achilles, the key to bringing down that impenetrable shield. The war that had ravaged our lands, claimed countless lives, and consumed our very souls would finally come to an end.

As I closed in on the shield, the grandeur of its presence became even more apparent. Its surface shimmered with an otherworldly glow, reflecting the rays of the sun like a thousand diamonds

With a steady hand, I raised the whistle to my lips and blew with all my might. The sound that emanated from the instrument was haunting, carrying a sense of urgency and divine plea. As the notes reverberated through the air, a cloud began to gather above, swirling and darkening the once clear sky.

The shield, once impenetrable, began to wane. Its ethereal glow flickered and faltered, revealing the vulnerability that lay beneath. With a surge of adrenaline, I tightened my grip on the spear, feeling its weight and power in my hands. This was the moment I had been waiting for, the chance to climb the walls and destroy the source of the shield's power once and for all.

Finally the war would end.

Finally Achilles would be free of this burden.

Finally we'd be together.

Suddenly, the world around me vanished into a dazzling white emptiness, leaving me feeling disoriented and bewildered. I found myself no longer in Troy, nor in the realm of mortals for that matter.

"Patroklos." From the depths of this desolation, a voice pierced the silence, causing me to startle. I turned abruptly, my eyes widening in surprise, to face the source of the sound. Standing there was a man, his presence both ethereal and unsettling. His long, brown hair cascaded down his back, mingling with his unkempt beard. His figure was emaciated, his body frail and fragile, as if a mere gust of wind could shatter his delicate form.

Fear and curiosity mingled within me as I cautiously addressed the mysterious figure. "Wh-Who are you?" I stammered, my voice barely above a whisper. The words hung in the air, echoing through the emptiness that surrounded us.

The man regarded me with eyes that seemed to hold a depth of knowledge and wisdom beyond comprehension. His gaze bore into my very soul, as if peering into the depths of my being. There was a weight to his presence, a sense of ancient power that emanated from him.

"I am the creator of the weapon that you are wielding," he announced, his voice echoing through the ancient void. My eyes widened in disbelief as I stared at the figure before me. Could it truly be the legendary Hephaestus?

"And before you ask, yes, I am still very much dead," he continued, his voice carrying a hint of amusement. "Right now, you are speaking with a...construct of myself."

I struggled to comprehend the magnitude of what he was saying. A construct? A mere projection of the god who had forged this weapon? It seemed impossible, yet here I stood, face to face with the mythical creator himself.

"Umm, alright...and how is it that we are speaking right now?" I managed to reply, my confusion evident in my voice.

Hephaestus regarded me with a knowing gaze, as if he could see the whirlwind of thoughts racing through my mind. "You have managed to unlock the spear's full potential," he explained, his tone filled with a mix of satisfaction and surprise. "The weapon was intended for Peleus' son, but it seems that you have mastered it before him."

"How? I was just about to win Troy for us, but I haven't done it yet. What great deed have I accomplished?" I questioned, my voice filled with confusion and curiosity.

"You are doing it for love," he said, his eyes gleaming with a depth of understanding that sent shivers down my spine. I looked at him, perplexed by his words. How could love be the key to my success?

"So many do things for glory, greed, power, lust. Selfishness! All of it is selfishness!" he suddenly burst out, his voice filled with a mix of frustration and bitterness. His outburst caught me off guard, and I couldn't help but feel a pang of sympathy for the pain he must have experienced.

He took a few deep breaths, his chest rising and falling with a sense of heaviness, before composing himself and continuing, "My mother never loved me. She only cared about my talent. My wife never loved me either. She'd rather fuck my brother and flaunt it to the world! My father had no time for me, consumed by his own desires. I only wanted someone to love me, that's why I created this weapon, Pandora. It is the greatest weapon I've ever created, and to unlock its full potential, the wielder must be fighting for love. For selflessness. That's why it chose you."

"So its true power comes from love?" I whispered, my voice filled with awe and disbelief.

Hephaestus nodded, his eyes gleaming with a profound under-standing. "It is strong enough to end your entire planet, if wielded with the purest form of love."

I stared at the weapon in my hand, its intricate design shimmering in the bright light. It was no longer just a tool of destruction, but a symbol of hope and redemption. The weight of responsibility settled upon my shoulders, both exhilarating and daunting.

"What should I do with it?" I asked, my voice trembling with anticipation.

Hephaestus paused for a moment, his gaze fixed on mine. "Finish what you started," he said, his voice filled with a quiet determination. "You want to end the war and be with your loved one forever? Then go, and do it."

With those words, a blinding light enveloped me, and when it faded, I found myself back at the very spot I had been before. The shield that had protected the city was now down, and the sounds of battle echoed in the distance behind me. Above me, I heard the sky crack open, as if unimaginable chaos was unfolding behind the dark clouds.

As I took a deep breath, the spear in my hand vibrated with an electric energy, as if it sensed the endless possibilities that lay before me. In that moment, a realization washed over me like a tidal wave. I didn't need to laboriously scale the towering wall that stood between me and victory. No, I possessed a power far greater than that of Achilles himself. With a surge of determination, I hurled the spear towards the city wall, its trajectory guided by a surge of raw energy. The impact was cataclysmic, creating a colossal hole in the wall. The resulting explosion sent debris hurtling through the air, showering the surroundings in a chaotic rain of destruction.

As the dust settled, a surge of exhilaration coursed through my veins. The horse beneath me galloped forward, its hooves pounding against the ground in a symphony of triumph. In that moment, I couldn't help but feel a surge of hope that the war, with its unending suffering and despair, would finally be brought to an end.

But my euphoria was abruptly shattered as a blinding light erupted from the heavens, searing through the air towards me with a malevolent intent. The force of the explosion engulfed me, leaving me disoriented and dazed. My vision blurred, my head throbbed with a relentless ache.

Struggling to regain my bearings, I found myself sprawled on the ground, the metallic tang of blood filling my senses. The horse, once a symbol of my triumph, now lay writhing on the earth, its lifeblood staining the ground crimson. Panic gripped me as I realized the extent of my injuries, my breath coming in ragged gasps, my heart pounding against the confines of my chest.

Frantically scanning the surroundings, my eyes darted in every direction, desperately seeking the spear that had slipped from my grasp. But it was as if the weapon had vanished into thin air, leaving me feeling vulnerable and defenseless.

As I continued to search, a figure materialized in the distance, slowly making its way towards me. My vision, still clouded and hazy, strained to discern the identity of this mysterious presence. But as the figure drew nearer, the details began to crystallize, revealing the unmistakable form of Apollo.

A brilliant light emanated from Apollo, casting an ethereal glow that seemed to transcend the boundaries of mortal perception. It bathed the surroundings in a mesmerizing luminescence, infusing the air with a sense of otherworldly power.

With deliberate grace, Apollo knelt down beside me, his touch gentle yet commanding as he grasped my chin, forcing my gaze to meet his piercing eyes.

His voice, resonating with a melodic quality, filled the air around us. "What a pity it is that you must meet your demise in this manner, gentle one," he intoned, his words carrying a weight of sorrow and regret. "In a different life, perhaps we'd be allies, fighting side by side against a common foe." And then, in a mere blink of eye, Apollo vanished from my sight, leaving me injured and alone.

The air crackled with tension as the cacophony of battle cries erupted behind me, the sound reverberating through the chaos of the battlefield. Slowly, my vision began to clear, revealing a sea of Trojans charging towards me with a relentless fury.

Ignoring the searing pain that radiated from my injured ankle, I summoned every ounce of strength and determination, adrenaline coursing through my veins. Limping with a determined resolve, I pushed forward, my mind solely fixated on retrieving the spear that lay just within reach.

But before I could reach my destination, a sudden whooshing sound sliced through the air, followed by a searing pain that lanced through my leg. My body instinctively crumpled to the ground, a guttural groan escaping my lips as the arrow found its mark. The agony threatened to overwhelm me, but I clung to the remnants of my willpower, crawling desperately towards the spear that held the key to my survival.

With each inch gained, the sound of approaching Trojan boots grew louder, their presence an imminent threat that spurred me on. I clawed at the earth, my hands bloodied and raw, the pain a mere afterthought compared to the urgency of the situation.

Finally, the spear lay within my grasp, its gleaming surface tauntingly close. But as my trembling fingertips reached out, a sudden jolt of excruciating pain shot through my hand, the tip of a Trojan spear piercing through my palm. A scream of anguish tore from my throat, mingling with the chaos of battle.

In the midst of my torment, a voice boomed above the clamor, cutting through the haze of agony. "You thought you could claim the city alone, Achilles?" Prince Hector's voice reverberated with a mixture of scorn and triumph. "What a fool you are!"

Summoning the last vestiges of my strength, fueled by a burning determination, I forced my other hand forward, fingers brushing against the cool metal of the spear. With a primal roar, I cried out the name that never left my thoughts, the name of the man who possessed half of my soul.

"ACHILLES!"

Chapter 22

T he darkness was all-encompassing, swallowing everything in its path. It felt the same as when I had encountered Hephaestus, but this time it was different. There was no sensation, no pain, no hunger, no thirst, and no warmth from the sun. I ran my hands over my body, searching for the wounds that had caused me so much pain, but there was nothing. I had been healed, but I felt empty, as if the very essence of life had been drained from me.

Suddenly, a mysterious figure materialized before me, emerging from the depths of the celestial realm. His presence was accompanied by an otherworldly speed, rendering him a blur of motion. Adorned with wings upon his helmet and shoes, the identity of this enigmatic being became clear - Hermes, the illustrious messenger of the gods.

"Grab my hand, soldier," Hermes' voice was gentle, his words filled with compassion. "It's time for your reward."

A wave of uncertainty washed over me, causing me to hesitate. My heart yearned to remain here, to reunite with Achilles, for he was my solace and strength.

"You have no shell to go back to, soldier," Hermes spoke softly. "Your body has no more life force. It's time to rest and cherish the reward The Judges have given you."

He took my hand and pulled me along with him. Reality seemed to warp and tear at his speed until we reached a giant, pale gate that stood in stark contrast to the darkness around us. Light radiated from behind the gate, and when it opened, I was blinded by its intensity.

As my eyes adjusted, I realized that everything had transformed. The sky was vibrant and full of life, the grass beneath my feet was soft and comforting, the air I breathed filled me with vitality, and the scent of it all was like a balm to my soul.

It was magical, but as I surveyed my surroundings, a profound realization washed over me, leaving me with a sense of desolation. There was an undeniable void, an emptiness that gnawed at my very core, leaving me with an indescribable feeling of incompleteness.

In this celestial sanctuary, it was the duty of Hermes himself to usher the souls of heroes and the valiant to their eternal rest. However, in my case, he had only brought half of my essence, leaving me in a state of profound anguish. This was meant to be my paradise, my sanctuary, but it had transformed into a personal hell. Without the presence of Achilles, my soul remained fragmented, forever yearning for its missing counterpart.

The fierce battle had finally come to an end, leaving behind a haunting scene of devastation. The once pristine sandy land was now littered with the lifeless bodies of hundreds of fallen soldiers. Their lifeless forms lay scattered across the desolate battlefield, a grim testament to the brutality of war. Despite the overwhelming loss of life, a palpable tension hung in the air, signaling that the conflict was far from resolved.

Inside his tent, Achilles, paced restlessly, his mind consumed by worry and fear. Every fiber of his being was focused on one person - Patroklos. Thoughts of Patroklos' safety consumed him, leaving no room for any other consideration.

Suddenly, the stillness of the tent was shattered as Achilles' spear pierced through the fabric, embedding itself forcefully into the sandy ground. His heart skipped a beat, hope surging through his veins as he anticipated Patroklos' arrival. Prayers and pleas to the gods spilled from his lips, desperate for his beloved friend to walk through that opening. But his hope was shattered as he realized it was only his spear, devoid of the presence he longed for.

Without a moment's hesitation, Achilles burst out of his tent in a frenzy, his voice echoing through the camp as he screamed and bellowed for Patroklos. The remaining soldiers, battle-worn and weary, watched him with a mixture of awe and pity, their eyes reflecting the weight of the loss he was experiencing.

"Achilles!" King Menelaus' voice echoed through the silence that covered the land. He was carrying the body of Patroklos in his arms, disposed of Achilles' armor and covered in blood.

Amidst the chaos, King Menelaus' voice cut through the air, commanding attention. The king cradled the lifeless body of Patroklos in his arms, stripped of Achilles' gleaming armor, now stained and matted with the dark crimson of blood. His expression was solemn, a reflection of the profound sorrow that enveloped the scene.

With a heavy heart, Menelaus gently passed the lifeless form to a heartbroken Achilles. The golden-haired boy sank to his knees, his body trembling as a quiet sob escaped his lips. He clutched

Patroklos' motionless body against his chest, his fingers tracing the contours of a face that would never again light up with life. The weight of grief pressed down upon him, threatening to suffocate him, rendering him speechless and incapable of finding words to express the depths of his pain.

Menelaus watched Achilles with a mixture of pity and sorrow, understanding the depth of his anguish. Though Agamemnon mirrored the same emotions, he couldn't help but let a small smirk slip from his lips. He knew that this devastating loss would be enough to drive Achilles back into his service, to aid him once again in the ongoing war.

Achilles had sought solace within the sacred confines of the temple, shutting himself off from the outside world. He had chosen this place, for he knew how much Patroklos cherished the sanctuary it offered, and perhaps, in some desperate hope, he believed that it could breathe life back into his fallen lover.

The floor was littered with shattered vials of ambrosia, their miraculous contents wasted in a futile attempt to revive Patroklos. Achilles had poured every drop of the healing nectar into his beloved, desperately hoping for a miracle. But in the end, not even the blood of a Goddess, could bridge the gap between life and death, leaving Achilles with nothing but shattered dreams and a heart heavy with grief.

Thetis knelt beside Achilles, her motherly presence bringing a sense of both comfort and sorrow. Her voice was soft, carrying the weight of a mother's love and understanding. "My little soldier," she whispered, her words laced with a profound sadness. "How it breaks my heart to witness your tears. I know the pain you endure, but you must release him. He needs the peace of eternal rest."

Achilles' anguish erupted in a raw cry of denial. "No!" he bellowed, his voice echoing through the hallowed space. "He is not gone! The ambrosia will work, and he will return to me!"

Thetis, her eyes filled with a mixture of love and sorrow, gently placed a hand on Achilles' trembling shoulder. "Oh, my dear child," she murmured, her voice filled with a mother's tenderness. "He has already crossed into the Elysian Fields. I sense no trace of his soul within his cold body. He is gone. Now, my love, you must let him rest."

Tears streamed down Achilles' face, his heart shattered by the realization that he would never again see his beloved in the mortal realm. The weight of this truth bore down upon him, a crushing agony that threatened to consume him entirely.

In this moment of profound grief, Achilles finally comprehended the true meaning behind Patroklos' words. The pursuit of glory and immortality had been his driving force, an obsession that not even his love for Patroklos could deter. But as he held his lifeless lover in his arms, Achilles finally understood the bitter irony. Death, far from being glorious, was a cruel and pitiful fate.

As the moon rose high in the sky, casting its ethereal glow upon the funeral pyre, the atmosphere grew heavy with grief and reverence. The crackling flames danced and leaped, devouring the wooden structure and engulfing Patroklos' lifeless body in a fiery embrace. The scent of burning wood mingled with the sweet aroma of incense, creating an otherworldly ambiance that seemed to bridge the gap between the mortal realm and the divine.

The haunting chants of the Myrmidons reverberated through the still night air, their voices carrying the weight of sorrow and loss. Achilles, his face streaked with tears, stepped forward with

Patroklos' bracelet clutched tightly in his hand. The powerful flame of the pyre illuminated his anguished expression, casting shadows upon his chiseled features. As he approached the pyre, his voice joined the chorus, resonating with a raw intensity that surpassed the others. Every word he sang was filled with a profound love and longing for his fallen lover.

The tears that streamed down Achilles' face seemed endless, their warmth mingling with the cool night air. But despite the intense heat emanating from the roaring pyre, he felt no physical sensation. His entire being was consumed by grief, his heart shattered into a million pieces that could never be made whole again.

Amidst the somber atmosphere, the soldiers of both Sparta and Myrmidon sought solace in the celebration of Patroklos' life. They danced and feasted, their movements a bittersweet tribute to the fallen hero. Some approached Achilles, their expressions filled with sympathy and condolences, but he remained oblivious to their presence. His eyes were fixed on the rising flames, his focus solely on the ashes that would soon soar into the night sky, carrying Patroklos' spirit to the realm of the gods.

Agamemnon approached Achilles with a solemn expression. His voice, though tinged with a hint of formality, held a genuine note of empathy. "I'm very sorry for your loss, dear friend," he offered, his words laced with sincerity.

Achilles' gaze remained fixed on the pyre, unyielding and uninterested in the king's words. "I'm not your 'dear friend,' King," he growled with contempt. "Leave me to my sorrow."

Agamemnon, undeterred by Achilles' hostility, continued speaking, his voice filled with understanding. "I understand the pain you're going through right now, young Prince. I too have experienced the heart-wrenching fear of losing a loved one. When my brother was struck down by that arrow, I thought I had lost him forever. But the Gods intervened and protected him."

Achilles felt a slight easing of tension in his face as the King of Sparta spoke, his voice carrying a rare sincerity that resonated within the young prince.

"It was that Trojan scum, Hector," Agamemnon's voice dripped with disdain as he uttered the name. "He shot him and betrayed the duel, a cowardly and unhonourable act. I'm sure you remember it well."

"It was Hector who murdered Patroklos!" Agamemnon continued, his gaze locked with Achilles'. "Many of our soldiers witnessed it."

Achilles' eyes blazed with a fiery intensity, the sorrow transforming into a seething rage within his heart. Agamemnon's words echoed through his mind, each syllable igniting a burning desire for vengeance. The name Hector reverberated within him, a symbol of the one who had torn his soul in half. It was clear to Achilles that Hector would pay for his heinous act, and pay dearly. No force on earth or in the heavens would be able to protect him from the wrath of Achilles.

With a steely determination etched into his features, Achilles turned away from Agamemnon, his gaze now fixed on the burning pyre. The flames danced and crackled, mirroring the fire that raged within his heart.

Chapter 23

Achilles had spent a sleepless night, tormented by the presence of two names that held contrasting emotions within him. One name, filled with love, brought bittersweet memories, while the other, dripping with disdain, ignited a fire of anger within his soul that could not be satisfied.

As the first rays of sunlight began to pierce through the tent, Achilles knew that the time had come. The soldiers around him slowly stirred from their slumber, awakening alongside the rising sun. With determination etched on his face, Achilles reached out and grasped his spear, its gleaming surface now adorned with Patroklos' dice bracelet, tightly wound around its shaft. With each step he took towards the city, the weight of those two names lingered heavily in his thoughts, like an unwelcome burden.

Some soldiers, aware of his purpose, trailed behind him at a distance, silently acknowledging the gravity of his mission. A few Myrmidons, who happened to be nearby, approached Achilles, their eyes filled with a mixture of concern and determination. They offered their assistance, eager to stand by his side, but he declined their offer, knowing that this was a task he had to undertake alone.

Achilles' grip tightened around his spear as he marched forward, his heart pounding with a fierce determination. As he reached the outskirts of the city, he brought his spear crashing down onto the ground with such force that the sound reverberated through the serene dawn, shattering the tranquility of the morning. In that moment, it felt as if the world around him ceased to exist, and he was transported into an unknown realm of nothingness. All he could perceive was an overwhelming expanse of blinding white, engulfing his senses.

Suddenly, a figure materialized before Achilles, his presence evoking little interest from the warrior. The man's long beard concealed most of his hideous face, while his unkempt hair cascaded down his back, partially obscuring his hunched posture. With a voice that carried an air of ancient wisdom, the man greeted Achilles, "Hello Peleus' son."

Achilles, his face twisted with anger and determination, forcefully confronted the figure standing in his path. His voice dripped with defiance as he spat out his words, "Step aside, God. I care not for your message. Hector will meet his demise at my hands today."

"And indeed, he shall," the man before him declared, his gaze unwavering. "I am Hephaestus, and as you are well aware, that gleaming spear in your hand is my creation."

Achilles squinted at the god, his confusion mingling with his rage. His voice laced with skepticism, he questioned, "Aren't you supposed to be dead?"

Hephaestus, his tone matter-of-fact and tinged with a hint of detachment, acknowledged Achilles' disbelief. "Indeed, you are correct. This form you see before you is a mere semblance of my true self, a projection. Recently, I had a conversation with your beloved companion as well... and if you stand here now, facing me in this manner, it can only mean that he too has met his tragic end."

Achilles' eyes suddenly burst with life, his entire being ignited at the mention of Patroklos. His voice trembled with urgency as he bombarded the god with questions, his words tumbling out in rapid succession. "You've met Patroklos?! When? How?"

Hephaestus, his gaze fixed upon the gleaming spear in Achilles' hand, began to reveal the truth. "The power of this very spear lies in the depths of love, and it was your dear Patroklos who tapped into its full potential before you did. In that moment, as he fought valiantly, our paths intertwined and we engaged in conversation."

"So that's why I couldn't harness its power until Patroklos helped me...the spear felt our love." His words hung in the air, heavy with the weight of revelation. Yet, a cloud of despair began to cast its shadow over his features, his voice growing deeper and tinged with a simmering hatred. "But now, he is gone, and the love I once felt seems to have vanished as well."

"Do not be mistaken, Prince. You are still fighting for love, but it has transformed into a different kind." Hephaestus explained his voice resonating with a gentle authority. "What you are experiencing now is grief...and what is grief if not the profound longing for the love you once held so dear."

Achilles locked eyes with the god, his expression shifting from confusion to a newfound clarity. In that moment, he comprehended the depth of Hephaestus' words, recognizing the truth they held. If love was the source of his strength, then grief, with its relentless ache, would transform him into an unstoppable force.

In an instant, Achilles was thrust back into reality, his surroundings transforming into the towering walls of Troy. With a surge of determination coursing through his veins, he planted his spear forcefully into the earth, its impact reverberating through the ground and causing a subtle tremor to ripple beneath his feet.

"HECTOR!!" Achilles bellowed with a ferocity that threatened to rend his vocal cords asunder. The sound of his voice echoed through the air, carrying his unyielding rage and consuming the land. Again and again, he repeated the name, each syllable dripping with a potent mix of fury and anguish. His desperate cries seemed to pierce the very fabric of reality, until, after a few agonizing moments, a figure emerged through the gaping hole in the gigantic walls of Troy.

Hector, adorned in Achilles' resplendent golden armor, stood before the barrier, his form illuminated by the brilliant rays of sunlight that cascaded upon the battlefield. A profound stillness settled between the two warriors as their eyes locked, a silent understanding passing between them, each aware of the imminent clash that would determine their fates.

"Listen to me Achilles," Hector began, his voice tinged with a mix of remorse and desperation. "I thought it was you that I killed yesterday and when I realised that it wasn't, I allowed your people to take your friend's body. We let you have a funeral and say farewell to him as a warrior. Please know that it was not my intent to hurt him, and I am very sorry. I too am mourning him."

Achilles, his face contorted with a mixture of disbelief and bitter disdain, let out a chilling chuckle that reverberated through the air. His unwavering gaze bore into Hector, fueled by a seething anger that threatened to consume him entirely. "You expect me to believe your words?" he sneered, his voice dripping with contempt. "You have no idea what you took from me...and now you dare stand in front of me wearing MY ARMOR! AND TELLING ME THAT YOU MOURN HIM ASWELL?!"

"I am aware that no words can undo the consequences of my actions," he murmured, his tone tinged with resignation. "But I implore you, do not unleash your wrath upon my people. Let your anger be directed solely at me."

The weight of the young life he had extinguished, a life filled with promise and potential, weighed heavily upon Hector's heart. As a warrior bound by honor, the etching lines of regret and sorrow upon his features were palpable.

"Then stop hiding behind that shield and face me like a man!" He thundered, his spear gripped tightly in his hand. With a swift motion, he kicked the base of his spear to the side, causing it to spin gracefully in his hand before he firmly anchored it beneath his armpit, his stance poised and ready for the impending clash.

Hector's gaze shifted momentarily to the towering walls of Troy, where the faces of his loved ones peered down at him, their eyes filled with a mixture of hope and trepidation.

Though his spirit longed for a peaceful resolution, Hector understood that the time for diplomacy had passed. The weight of responsibility pressed upon his shoulders, leaving him with no choice but to confront Achilles in battle.

Deep down, Hector knew the odds were stacked against him. Yet, even in the face of insurmountable odds, a flicker of hope burned within Hector's soul. If there existed even the slightest chance that he could emerge victorious, that he could save his beloved kingdom from the clutches of destruction, he would seize it without hesitation. For the sake of his people, his family, and the legacy of Troy, he would embrace the daunting challenge that lay before him.

Achilles, grew impatient as he paced restlessly across the battlefield, his eyes locked unwaveringly on the Prince. Each step he took seemed to reverberate with a simmering intensity, the ground trembling beneath his feet as he awaited Hector's emergence.

As soon as the Prince of Troy stepped beyond the protective barrier, Achilles launched himself forward with a thunderous surge of power. His movements were swift and purposeful, his spear slicing through the air with lethal precision. There was no hesitation, no moment of respite, as Achilles sought to strike down his adversary without a single moment's delay.

The clash of metal against metal echoed through the battlefield as Achilles' spear collided with Hector's shield. The impact reverberated through the air, causing the Prince to stagger backward, his balance momentarily compromised. Yet, even in the face of adversity, Hector's resilience shone through. With unwavering resolve, he quickly regained his balance, his muscles tensing like a tightly wound spring.

Hector's strikes came forth with a ferocity that mirrored the flames of his determination. Each movement was executed with a deadly precision, his sword slicing through the air like a serpent striking its prey. Yet, despite the Prince of Troy's skill and speed, Achilles remained an elusive target. Like a phantom, he effortlessly evaded each attack, his body moving with an otherworldly grace.

In the midst of the battle, memories flooded Achilles' mind, images of Patroklos, intertwining with the present. The sound of clashing swords and the heat of the sun-soaked sand beneath his feet transported him back to the days of their training, where Achilles would revel in showcasing his exceptional skills. But now, in this moment, the thrill and excitement that once coursed through his veins were absent, replaced by a hollow ache that echoed in the depths of his soul.

As Achilles shook the thought away, he found Hector charging towards him, his sword held high. In one swift motion, he disarmed Hector, knocking the sword from his grip, and delivered a powerful blow to his jaw.

Hector crumpled to the ground, the air heavy with anticipation as everyone in the vicinity held their breath. Achilles, his gaze fixed elsewhere, continued to walk nonchalantly around the fallen prince. His voice, devoid of any trace of triumph, resonated through the air. "Get up, Prince of Troy," he said, his tone laced with a mix of disdain and determination. "You won't be dying so easily today."

With Hector rising to his feet, determination etched into every line of his face, he launched himself forward in a desperate bid to reclaim his honor. But Achilles, ever the predator, swiftly countered, his movements calculated and precise. In a brutal display of superiority, he brought Hector crashing down to the ground once again, his body wracked with humiliation.

In the midst of the battle, Achilles' mind drifted back to a night long past, a night he had spent teaching Patroklos the art of adaptation. The memory brought a fleeting smile to his lips, a remnant of the playful joy he had once felt. But now, in this moment, that joy was replaced by a somber realization of the gravity of the situation.

The force of Hector's sword against Achilles' spear sent sparks cascading through the air. Hector fought with every ounce of his being, his strikes fueled by a fierce determination to defend his life, his honor, and his people. Yet, in stark contrast, Achilles stood before him, a figure of dominance and control. He toyed with Hector, like a predator toying with his prey. This was never a fair fight.

As the battle raged on, Hector's fatigue began to weigh heavily upon him. He knew that this fleeting moment would be his only chance to turn the tide. With a surge of desperation, he swung his sword with all his might, striking the ground beneath him. A cloud of sand erupted, obscuring Achilles' vision and causing him to instinctively shield his eyes.

Momentarily blinded, Achilles frantically searched for Hector amidst the swirling chaos. But before he could regain his bearings, a sudden swooshing sound jolted him from the side. Hector had seized the opportunity, hurling his shield at Achilles with a force born of desperation. Achilles, caught off guard, crouched instinctively, narrowly evading the incoming shield.

With unyielding determination, Hector charged at Achilles, his every muscle straining with the weight of his resolve. Achilles, still disoriented, managed to evade the majority of Hector's frenzied swings, his body moving with an otherworldly agility. But one strike slipped through his defenses, the tip of Hector's sword grazing Achilles' chest, leaving a shallow, stinging wound in its wake.

In that fleeting moment, a tremor seemed to ripple through the earth, as if even the mighty Poseidon, the earth shaker, watched with a mix of concern and anticipation.

Achilles stood frozen in disbelief, his mind reeling from the realization that he had been touched by an enemy's weapon. It was a sensation he had never experienced before, an intrusion upon his invincibility that felt almost surreal in its audacity.

But Hector, relentless in his pursuit, did not pause to savor the moment. He continued his assault, thrusting his sword towards

Achilles with unwavering determination. Sensing the urgency of the situation, Achilles swiftly planted the spear onto his neck, using it as a lever to push back against Hector's relentless advance. The spear jutted out towards Hector, creating temporary distance and buying Achilles a precious moment to gather his thoughts.

Hector, ever astute, recognized Achilles' ploy. With a quick and calculated parry, he deflected the spear, seizing the opportunity to strike Achilles directly in the face with a powerful punch. The force of the blow sent Achilles stumbling backward, his head spinning from the impact.

With the taste of victory within his grasp, Hector lunged forward to deliver the finishing blow. But Achilles, though momentarily disoriented, summoned his remaining strength and managed to intercept the attack. Using the shaft of his spear as a makeshift shield, he blocked Hector's assault, narrowly averting disaster.

Yet, Hector's momentum was too great, his strength overpowering. In a desperate bid to regain control, Achilles instinctively reached out and grabbed hold of Hector, pulling him backwards with all his might. The sudden shift in balance caused both warriors to lose their footing, their bodies entangled as they tumbled to the unforgiving ground.

Both Hector and Achilles, their bodies weary and drained, summoned the last vestiges of their strength to rise from the ground. With aching muscles and labored breaths, they swung their weapons at each other in a final display of defiance. The clash of metal reverberated through the air as their blades collided, but in a cruel twist of fate, their weapons were knocked from their grasp.

Now stripped of their weapons, they were left with nothing but their bare fists as their only means of defense. Gone was the elegance, the finesse, and the skill that had once defined their duel. What remained was raw, unadulterated emotion, transforming the once noble contest into a pitiful brawl.

Reason and strategy had been abandoned, overshadowed by the overwhelming tide of their emotions. They fought with a reckless abandon, their minds consumed by a primal instinct to overpower their adversary at any cost.

Blow after blow rained down upon each other, a relentless barrage of strikes that blurred the line between pain and fury. The sound of flesh meeting flesh filled the air, punctuated by grunts and gasps of exertion. The intensity of their battle escalated, their bodies becoming a canvas of bruises and blood.

In a moment of sheer desperation, Hector managed to seize the upper hand. With a surge of strength, he pinned Achilles to the unforgiving ground, his hands closing tightly around Achilles' throat. The weight of Hector's grip constricted Achilles' airway, his breaths coming in desperate gasps as darkness threatened to engulf his vision.

As his consciousness wavered on the precipice of surrender, Achilles closed his eyes, surrendering to the impending peace that beckoned him. Amidst the encroaching darkness, a faint echo of a voice reached his ears, a voice that stirred a deep and indelible memory within him, a voice he could never forget.

"You killed me," the voice seethed with a venomous aggression that pierced Achilles' soul. "Your hubris, your arrogance, it killed me. You had the power to be a hero, to save me from this fate, but you chose yourself above all else."

Achilles' voice shattered into fragments, his words barely audible through the weight of his remorse. "I'm sorry... I'm so sorry!" he pleaded, his voice trembling with a mixture of anguish and desperation. "Please, Patroklos, forgive me! I just want to hold you again!"

The memories flooded back, assaulting Achilles' senses with a bittersweet intensity. He could almost taste the tranquility that enveloped them as they sat under the shade of that ancient tree, their laughter mingling with the gentle melodies of the lyre. The wind whispered secrets in their ears, carrying their harmonious voices across the fields.

His heart quickened as he recalled the tender moments when their fingers intertwined, their touch electric with a love that defied the boundaries of this mortal realm. The anticipation that coursed through his veins when Patroklos leaned against his chest, their bodies fitting together like pieces of a puzzle, ignited a fire within his core.

Oh, how Achilles would give anything to turn back time, to relive those stolen moments of bliss. But the cruel reality of life's transience crashed upon him like a relentless wave. The past slipped through his fingers like sand, forever out of reach.

"Achilles' voice trembled, barely audible, as he whispered into the void, "Just let me die... so I can be with you again." His words hung heavy in the air, a desperate plea to reunite with the one he had lost.

But the voice, relentless and unforgiving, refused to grant him solace. "You said you'd avenge me," it echoed with a haunting intensity. "True heroes keep their promises. So kill him... Wake up, and KILL HIM! WAKE UP, WAKE UP!" The voice grew louder, more urgent, as if urging Achilles to awaken from his slumber of grief and exact the vengeance he had sworn.

As the voice faded into the distance, swallowed by the vast expanse of Achilles' consciousness, a blinding light pierced through the darkness. Slowly, the world around him materialized once more, drawing him back into the brutal reality of the battle that raged on.

Summoning the last remnants of his strength, Achilles reached out, his hand trembling as it made contact with Hector's chest. Hector, confusion etched across his face, met Achilles' gaze, unaware of the impending doom that awaited him. Time seemed to stand still as Achilles' spear pierced itself through Hector's heart.

A gasp escaped Hector's lips, his hand instinctively grasping the weapon. Slowly, as the life faded from his eyes, Hector dropped to the floor,

Achilles rose to his feet, his towering figure casting a shadow over the fallen Hector. He reached down and retrieved his gauntlet, the gleaming golden armor that adorned his body, the very symbol of his invincibility. As he fastened it back into place, the armor seemed to meld seamlessly with his form, becoming one with him and rebuilding its damaged self.

With a solemn determination, Achilles grasped the hilt of his spear, still embedded in Hector's lifeless body. The sound of metal scraping against flesh filled the air as he withdrew the weapon, its sharp tip stained crimson with the blood of his fallen foe. In a calculated motion, he thrust the spear into Hector's leg.

Achilles' hand, steady and unwavering, hovered above the spear for a moment, his eyes fixed upon it. With a single touch, a surge of energy coursed through the weapon, propelling it with a force that defied reason. The spear, now free from Achilles' grasp, soared through the air, slicing through the battlefield with a deadly precision. It disappeared into the distance, its trajectory leading it back to the Greek camp, dragging Hector's lifeless body behind it with a violent force.

As the echoes of the spear's departure faded into the distance, Achilles turned his gaze towards the city of Troy, its walls standing tall and defiant. He drank in the sight one last time, his eyes filled with a mixture of hatred and sorrow. The weight of the war, the lives lost, and the choices made, bore down upon him with an almost tangible heaviness.

Chapter 24

Hector's body hang from a wooden cross as crows had already gathered around it, gnawing at his flesh. His face and chest had already been massacred from being dragged back to camp with the full force of Achilles' spear, which made it impossible to even recognise that it was him at all.

Achilles remained isolated within his tent. He had hoped that this pain, this longing, would have disappeared once he had killed Hector, yet here still it remained. It was all he could think about and he finally came to a conclusion.

He decided that he was going to kill himself. To release his soul from this agony. He wanted to see Patroklos again so badly that he had forgotten that to enter Elysium he'd have to complete a heroic deed and he had yet to capture Troy for the Spartans.

With this fact shrouded amidst his excruciating thoughts, Achilles clasped his spear tightly within his palm, its sharp edge pressed against his neck. But as he was about to end it once and for all, a man entered his tent unannounced.

"You killed my son just so you can also do it to yourself?" The old man spoke, his voice full of spite and melancholia. "Is human life that meaningless to you?!"

Achilles took a good glance at the man and he knew exactly who he was looking at. King Priam was in his tent, the father of Hector. He had somehow managed not to get spotted on his way here.

"Your son got what he deserved. He murderer my soul, my agape." Achilles grumbled, as each word spat out like lava. "I hope the Erinyes are torturing him endlessly in the depths of Tartarus."

"You think my son a monster, but you are the only one here!" Priam was outraged, unable to contain himself from Achilles' insults. "You, Greeks, showed up to our home and declared war upon my homeland, you massacred my people, you butchered my son, and now you want to play victim?!"

"You did this to yourselves. You took Helen from her husband and broke the treaty. If your son wasn't such a moron, maybe all of this would had been avoided." Achilles turned away from the King, as if he had gotten uninterested.

"That, at least we can agree on." The King said abruptly, causing Achilles to turn his attention back on him. "My young one is madly in love he says. So mad that he didn't think his actions would cause a war."

King Priam rubbed his hand across his face and beard and let out an exhausting sigh as he continued, "But Hector was a good man." He stated with undevoted determination. "My son had honor, and he had a big heart. When he killed that boy, he was devastated. He came and cried to me about how young he was -- and HELL! -- so are you! Hector wanted to make it right by you, but he knew you wouldn't change your mind. We all knew, but he was the only one who hoped you would. We told him to not fight you, but he did anyways because it was the only way to stop you from annihilating the city. He sacrificed himself for all of us. For me, for his family, for our people, for his idiotic brother who caused all of this. HE WAS A GOOD MAN, AND YOU TOOK HIM FROM US!!"

Achilles gazed at Priam, unable to think of what to say. What could he even say after all that?

And so King Priam, sniffing and rubbing his tears, resumed, "All I've been witnessing is people killing each other because of love. But that is not what love is, that's not what it ever should be. So I've come to ask you to return my son's body to me. Even in his deformed state, I wish to give a proper burial just like you did with your love one. He deserved that much, and if my blabbering hasn't convince even the tiny bit of humanity that's still left in you to do this, then you will have to kill me as well. I leave the choice up to you."

Achilles was stunned at the King's words. It was as if he had a revelation, and just finally realised that his fury and thirst for vengeance caused so much pain that he was blind to.

Achilles was always fine with killing people, if they were a threat then he'd slaughter them with no second thought. But Patroklos was the one who saw the best in everyone. Even if they had done wrong or caused harm, he'd find a way to make them appear human.

And as Priam explained his side of the story, Achilles finally realised he had turned himself into the very thing he saw others as. In that moment, Achilles remembered Patroklos telling him that even the worst of people deserve a second chance, and so he took it upon himself to atone for what he had done.

"I will return your son's body, King." Achilles approached the King and kneeled before him, grasping his hand and pressing his lips against it. "Please, forgive me for what I've taken from you..."

King Priam gazed at him with a hint of disdain and sorrow, and said, "I will not forgive you. If you want forgiveness, then you must ask it from within yourself and accomplish something good with your life. That's how you'll earn the forgiveness your soul so desperately desires."

Chapter 25

In the eerie silence that lingered over the land, the aftermath of the Gods' cataclysmic battle echoed. Since that unforgettable clash, the divine figures had withdrawn into an ominous silence, leaving behind a world ravaged by their strife.

Amidst the darkened night, the Trojans gathered to honor their fallen prince, Hector, in a solemn burial rite. Lord Priam, Prince Paris, Lady Helen, and Hector's wife, Andromache stood by, gazing mournfully at Hector's pyre as it consumed his mortal remains.

In this moment of profound sorrow, a sudden calamity shattered what little hope lingered. A lightning bolt, as if hurled from the heavens, struck the heart of the protective shield, shattering the technology that sustained the barrier. The dawn of the end seemed imminent.

Chaos erupted as the Trojans scrambled to arm themselves, rallying atop the city walls, prepared to defend their homeland. Years spent behind the protective barrier hadn't dulled their instincts; defending their city was ingrained in their very beings.

However, a glaring issue persisted-the breach in the wall.

The Greeks, taken aback by the spectacle, wasted no time. Agamemnon and Menelaus swiftly marshaled their forces, launching an immediate assault on the city.

Amidst the turmoil, the soldiers' faces lit up with an unfamiliar sense of anticipation; it was as though they sensed the impending conclusion of the war, the chance to finally reunite with their loved ones back home.

Cannonballs and arrows streaked across the night sky, clashing against the Greek forces. Yet, their resolve remained unshaken; they knew this had to be the final confrontation, and they were ready to face whatever challenges lay ahead.

Through the deserted camp, Achilles raced toward Agamemnon's tent. A guard, startled by Achilles' sudden appearance, attempted to speak, only to be swiftly rendered unconscious by a single blow from Achilles.

Inside the tent, Achilles was met with a chilling sight. Briseis lay bound on the ground, her clothes torn and bloodied, her face bearing the marks of brutality.

As Achilles approached Briseis, his heart sank at the sight of the dark, angry bruises marring her delicate skin. He reached out to touch them, but before he could, Briseis's eyes snapped open and she grabbed his arm with a fierce strength.

"Why are you here?" Her voice was filled with disdain, her eyes blazing with a fury that matched his own.

"Your people don't deserve any of this," Achilles said, his voice heavy with regret as he used his spear to cut through the ropes binding her hands. "I can't undo what I've done, but I will do everything in my power to help you, for as long as I live."

For a moment, Briseis's fiery gaze softened as she looked into Achilles's deep, ocean-colored eyes.

"I'm sorry about Patroklos," she said softly. "He was good."

"He was." Achilles agreed.

With a solemn offering of truce, Achilles extended his arm to her. Briseis regarded it for a heartbeat before placing her hand in his. He gripped her gently and helped her rise, pulling her up from the cold, unforgiving ground into a stand of solidarity.

"I want you to have this." Achilles' voice was imbued with a solemn gravity as he reached around the sturdy leather belt cinched at his waist, his fingers closing around the cool metal of a silver-sheathed spear. With a deliberate motion, he presented it to her. "It was Patroklos', I think he'd want you to have it."

Briseis' hands trembled slightly as she accepted the sheathed weapon, her fingers brushing against the intricate engravings that adorned its surface. As she gripped it, her touch inadvertently triggered a mechanism, and the spear extended with a swift, fluid motion to its full, formidable length. The sudden transformation startled her, sending a shiver of surprise through her arms and causing her to take an involuntary step back.

A light, affectionate laugh escaped Achilles as he watched her reaction, the sound warm in the cool air. Briseis shot him a quick, reproachful look, her brows knitting together in a frown that didn't quite reach her eyes.

"Patroklos had the very same reaction the first time," Achilles said, his smile tinged with nostalgia as he lost himself for a moment in the bittersweet memories of his beloved comrade.

He pointed to a small, unassuming button on the spear's shaft. "This is what controls the transformation. Press it, and the spear will shift from a compact rod back to its extended form. Aside from that, it functions just as any other spear would." His explanation was thorough, ensuring she understood the weapon's unique feature.

Briseis nodded, her expression hardening with resolve as she mentally rehearsed the mechanism. "Understood. Now let's go kill that son of a bitch."

With a shared sense of purpose, they turned away from the relative safety of their encampment. Together, they strode with determined pace toward the city, where plumes of smoke rose and the distant roar of flames and chaos signalled the battle that awaited them.

Chapter 26

In the midst of the raging inferno, the air thick with the acrid smell of smoke and charred flesh, lay the lifeless bodies of the innocent. Husbands, mothers, sisters, brothers, and lovers - all once filled with laughter and joy, now lay motionless, their vacant eyes staring blankly into the abyss. The screams of the tormented still echoed through the air, a haunting reminder of the brutality that had unfolded.

Briseis, resplendent in Patroklos' gleaming silver armor, stood frozen, her pupils dilated in horror as she gazed upon the massacred bodies. Her eyes locked onto theirs, searching for a flicker of life, but all she found was vacant, lifeless stares.

With a guttural roar, Briseis clenched her fist so tightly that her knuckles turned white, as if she could physically wring out the anguish that coursed through her veins. "Fucking monsters!" she bellowed, her voice hoarse with rage, the words torn from the very depths of her being.

Achilles, his eyes blazing with a fierce determination, placed a hand on her shoulder, his massive frame a reassuring presence amidst the devastation. "They'll get what they deserve," his voice low and menacing. "Come, we mustn't stop now. We have to see this through to the end."

Achilles and Briseis navigated the blazing streets with caution, their footsteps deliberate and silent, as they sought to avoid detection by the rampaging Spartan forces.

As they turned a corner, they stumbled upon a scene of unmitigated horror. Trojan civilians, their faces etched with terror, were being herded into a makeshift execution line, their hands bound behind their backs.

No words were needed between Achilles and Briseis; their thoughts were in tandem, their hearts burning with rage and indignation. Without hesitation, they sprang into action, their actions fueled by a primal urge to protect the helpless, and rushed headlong into the fray to intervene.

Achilles unleashed his spear with a mighty roar, the razor-sharp tip slicing through the air to impale two Spartan soldiers, their bodies crumpling to the ground as the shaft lodged deep within their chests. Before the stunned remnants of the squad could even flinch, Achilles summoned his spear back to his hand with a flick of his wrist.

With the Spartans' attention fully enthralled by Achilles' tempestuous charge, Briseis seized the momentary distraction to strike, her slender spear flashing in the flickering light of the burning city as she plunged it deep into the back of an unsuspecting soldier. The man's eyes widened in shock, his mouth frozen in a silent scream, as he collapsed to the ground, lifeless.

This was the first time Briseis had taken a life, yet the act didn't stir even a whisper of remorse within her. These soldiers had brought ruin to her people, razed her city, and shattered her existence forever. As she gazed down at the lifeless form, all she felt was an echoing emptiness, a hollow numbness that seemed to consume her very soul.

A swift sword stroke sliced through the air, mere inches from Briseis' face, and she raised her arm just in time to deflect the blow, the weapons clashing with a loud ring. The attacker's companion seized the opportunity to strike, and Briseis, unable to fend off both assailants simultaneously, stumbled backward under the relentless onslaught. The final blow sent her crashing to the ground, her back slamming against the cold, unforgiving ground.

Dazed and disoriented, Briseis scanned her surroundings, her gaze frantically searching for Achilles. She found him engulfed in a whirlwind of clashing steel, his imposing figure at the center of a maelstrom of five skilled warriors. His movements were a blur of precision and power, each stroke a masterclass in deadly elegance.

A pang of envy pricked at Briseis' heart, a yearning to wield a weapon with such grace and assurance. Yet, she knew her limitations - her lack of training, her novice skills, and her frailty compared to the battle-hardened warriors around her. The weight of her vulnerability threatened to crush her, but she refused to yield. In this unforgiving world, adaptation was the key to survival, and Briseis steeled herself to confront her weaknesses head-on.

She was a diminutive figure amidst the towering warriors, but her compact frame proved to be an advantage, allowing her to dart and weave with an agility that belied her tender years. With a swift press of a button, her armor dissolved into nothingness, freeing her from its cumbersome weight. One of the soldier's attacks came crashing down, a blur of steel and fury, but Briseis sidestepped the blow with ease, her lithe body rolling nimbly to the side as she regained her footing.

In an instant, both Spartans closed in, their swords converging from opposing directions like deadly pinchers. Briseis' heart raced as she realized she had no escape route, no way to dodge this pincer movement. But in a flash of inspiration, she summoned her armor back into being, the Myrmidon suit materializing around her like a shimmering aura. The armor's gleaming plates slid into place, encasing her body in a protective shell just as the twin attacks landed.

One blow struck her back, the force of the impact sending jolts of pain coursing through her spine like electric shocks. But the armor held fast, its metal plates absorbing the brunt of the attack, sparing her from the worst of the damage. The second attack was blocked by her outstretched arm, the sword clashing against her spear with a loud clang. Her vision blurred momentarily, but she refused to yield. She was alive, and that was all that mattered.

Just as the soldier behind her was going for another attack, a Trojan citizen, fueled by desperation and fury, launched himself at the attacker, tackling him to the ground with a fierce cry. The sudden reversal of fortune gave Briseis the opening she needed.

With lightning-quick reflexes, she whipped her spear around, the tip biting deep into the chest armor of the soldier standing before her. The force of the blow sent shockwaves through his body, and he stumbled back, groaning in agony as the air wheezed from his lungs. For an instant, he was vulnerable, and Briseis seized the chance to deliver the killing blow. However, her opponent recovered with a speed that belied his wounded state, and he parried her strike with a swift motion. The clash of their weapons sent sparks flying in all directions, illuminating the darkening streets like tiny stars.

With a vicious snarl, the soldier slapped her across the face, the force of the blow sending her crashing to the ground. As she struggled to regain her footing, both Spartans closed in, their faces twisted into wicked grins. Briseis' gaze darted behind her, where she saw the lifeless body of the Trojan citizen who had briefly come to her aid.

"No!" Briseis' anguished cry echoed through the ravaged streets as the soldiers loomed over her, their weapons poised to deliver the final blow. But before their blades could even begin their deadly arcs, a shocking detonation rocked the air. One of the soldiers' heads disintegrated into a gruesome mess of tissue and bone, his brain matter splattering Briseis like a macabre baptism. The warm, sticky liquid dripped from her hair, her skin, and her armor, leaving her covered in the detritus of war.

His stunned comrade froze, paralyzed by the horror of it all, his eyes wide with terror as his gaze locked onto the unrecognizable remains of his fallen companion. Before he could even register the full gravity of his situation, Achilles' spear shot forth, its deadly tip piercing the air with precision, and cleaved through the skulls of both soldiers with ruthless efficiency.

Achilles strode forward, his powerful arm outstretched, his piercing gaze fixed on Briseis. She gazed up at him, her vision blurring through the crimson veil of gore that shrouded her face. With trembling hands, she accepted his offered arm, her fingers closing around his like a lifeline. A part of her seethed with frustration, wishing she could have been the one to mete out justice to her would-be executioners. Yet, a deeper, more primal gratitude swelled within her, directed at Achilles, her savior, who had intervened to spare her life in the nick of time.

"Are you alright?" Achilles' voice was laced with concern as he gazed down at Briseis, his piercing blue eyes scanning her blood-stained face and armor.

Her response was a defiant cry, torn from the depths of her soul. "No!" The word echoed through the ravaged streets, a testament to the anguish and desperation that had taken hold of her. "They are slaughtering my people like it's nothing, and I don't have the power to do anything about it." Her voice cracked, the weight of her helplessness threatening to crush her.

Achilles' gaze locked onto hers, and for an instant, he was transported back to the darkest moments of his own past. He saw the same burning fury, the same desperation that had driven him to madness after Patroklos' tragic demise. He understood the depths of her rage, the sense of impotence that came with being unable to protect those she loved.

Without a word, Achilles reached out and placed his arm on her shoulder, his grip firm and reassuring. His touch was like a balm to her ravaged soul, a reminder that she was not alone in this chaos.

"I don't know you," he began, his voice low and measured, "but I know you're brave. Braver than most people I know. You are here, fighting, and doing the best you can to save your people and your land, so don't put yourself down. You're more of a hero than I could ever be." The words were a gentle rebuke, a reminder that her courage in the face of overwhelming odds was something to be cherished, not diminished.

Briseis' gaze locked onto Achilles', and what she saw pierced her heart. Behind the legendary warrior's piercing blue eyes, she beheld a lost soul, tormented by the weight of his own guilt. The greatest hero of the age, feared by all, was in truth a fragile mortal, haunted by the shadows of his past mistakes. The realization that even mighty Achilles had vulnerabilities provided comfort to her wounded soul.

As she pondered this, Briseis' thoughts turned inward, and she realized that her own weaknesses did not define her. She might not possess the strength to vanquish the Spartans single-handedly, but she was brave. She had always been brave, from the moment she had defied her captors to protect her sister, to her attempts to slay Agamemnon, the man who had brought ruin to their city. Even when captured and broken, her spirit had refused to be crushed. The recognition of her own resilience brought a fierce determination to her eyes.

Without hesitation, Briseis reached out and grasped Achilles' hand, her fingers closing around his like a vice. "We both have our faults," she declared, her voice trembling with conviction, "but together, we will end this. We'll both become the heroes we desire to be." The words hung in the air, a promise of redemption and triumph.

With a nod of understanding, Achilles and Briseis released the captive citizens from their bonds, freeing them from their cruel fate. Together, the unlikely duo set their course towards the palace, their hearts beating as one in their quest for justice and vengeance.

Epilogue

Achilles and Briseis entered the palace, stepping over the lifeless bodies scattered on the floor, leading them deeper into the eerie silence within. The absence of any signs of life created a haunting atmosphere, emphasizing the emptiness of the once vibrant place.

Suddenly, a piercing scream shattered the stillness, propelling Achilles and Briseis up the staircase towards the source. As they emerged into the backyard, a tense confrontation unfolded before them. King Agamemnon, Menelaus, and a group of soldiers stood face to face with King Priam, Paris, and Helen. The lifeless form of Hector's beloved, Andromache, lay on the ground, a tragic witness to the unfolding chaos.

"You savages!" Lord Priam's voice thundered with anger and grief, his sword raised in defiance.

Paris, consumed by a storm of emotions, unleashed a fierce assault towards Agamemnon, driven by a mix of rage and desperation. The King's swift reflexes allowed him to deflect the attack, sending Paris crashing to the ground in a tumult of dust and debris.

"Finish him off, brother!" Agamemnon's commanding voice echoed through the chaos, urging Menelaus to deliver the final blow to Paris.

As the tension thickened in the air, Lady Helen's voice cut through the chaos like a beacon of reason and compassion. With a sense of urgency, she positioned herself between Menelaus and Paris, her words a plea for peace and sanity in the midst of the escalating conflict.

"Menelaus, please!" Her voice trembling. "This is not the path of kindness and honor you walk. Do not let that monster tarnish the light within you." Her eyes, filled with a mix of sorrow and resolve, locked onto Agamemnon with a raw display of pure disgust, condemning his ruthless thirst for bloodshed and vengeance.

Agamemnon's voice boomed with malice as he commanded his brother, his words dripping with venom and hatred. "Don't listen to this traitorous wench! This little shit caused all of this, brother! He took your wife and humiliated you! Kill him!" Menelaus, consumed by a fiery rage towards Paris, tightened his grip on his sword, his eyes fixed on the Prince with a deadly resolve.

In a swift and decisive move, Achilles sprang into action, his movements fluid and precise. With a fierce determination, he hurled his spear directly at Menelaus's raised sword, the impact shattering the blade in a resounding clash. Menelaus, frozen in disbelief, realized with a jolt how perilously close his hand had come to being severed off.

The golden spear continued its deadly trajectory with a deadly grace. It sliced through the air, piercing through the ranks of the twelve Spartan soldiers with a devastating force, bringing a sudden and tragic end to their lives in a swift and merciless strike.

With a fierce determination burning in her eyes, Briseis wasted no time in launching herself towards Agamemnon, driven by a deep-seated desire to bring an end to his life once and for all.

As the spear found its way back into Achilles' grasp, he approached Menelaus with a cautious yet resolute demeanor, their gazes locked in a silent exchange of tension and unspoken words.

"Stand down, Menelaus. I do not wish to bring harm upon you," Achilles's voice carried a tone of firm resolve, seeking to avoid further bloodshed.

Menelaus, unable to find words to match the turmoil within him, let his eyes convey the weight of his defeat and resignation. With a heavy heart, the King relinquished his broken sword, letting it fall to the ground with a clatter, before sinking to his knees in a gesture of surrender and acceptance of his fate.

"Just end it." Menelaus whispered softly.

Achilles, moved by a sense of compassion and understanding, knelt before the defeated King. Placing a reassuring hand on Menelaus's shoulder, Achilles spoke with a mix of empathy and respect.

"You were the only one brave enough to bring Patroklos' body back to me. I won't ever forget that. You are a man of honor who faltered in the grip of anger and love. Live on, King, and seek redemption for your choices," Achilles's words carried a weight of forgiveness and understanding. Having been in Menelaus's shoes before, he hoped to prevent another from succumbing to the same darkness.

Achilles rose to his feet as Helen approached to offer solace to the despondent Menelaus. She gave Achilles a slight smile, a sign of gratitude.

On the other side, Agamemnon's anguished cry pierced the air as Briseis, with a swift and daring move, managed to drive her blade into the King's thigh. However, her triumph was short-lived as Agamemnon seized her arm, swiftly unequipping the armor from her body, leaving her vulnerable and exposed before him.

Turning Briseis around, Agamemnon pressed his sword menacingly against her neck, halting Achilles in his tracks.

"What are you doing, brother!?" Agamemnon's voice thundered with tangible fury, his anger reverberating through the tense atmosphere. "Stand up and fight!"

Yet, Menelaus remained seated, a picture of utter defeat and resignation, his spirit broken by the ravages of war.

"Let her go...or I will end you in an instant." Achilles's voice carried a steely resolve, his spear poised and ready for action.

"Ah, but of course!" Agamemnon's demeanor swiftly shifted to his customary cunning and mocking tone. "The little warrior relies solely on his mighty spear! A coward's weapon, indeed."

Achilles was keenly aware of Agamemnon's manipulative tactics, understanding that the King's only chance of victory lay in playing on Achilles's emotions. Despite this knowledge, Achilles chose to play along, not out of concern for his honor or the need to prove his prowess as a warrior, but rather out of a deeper drive to embody the role of a hero. Being the hero meant making sacrifices, even at great personal cost. This was the path he had to tread in order to be reunited with his beloved once more.

"I challenge you to a duel," Achilles declared, his voice ringing with authority as he sent his spear soaring into the sky with a display of formidable strength. "No divine weapons..." With a deliberate motion, he shed his armor and cast his gauntlet across the yard.

"...no deceit, just a battle of honor between us. If you emerge victorious, Troy is yours. But should I prevail, you will lead your army back to Sparta and never set foot on this soil again."

The terms of the challenge heavily favored Agamemnon, ensuring his survival regardless of the outcome. Achilles understood the gravity of the offer and knew that Agamemnon could not afford to reject it.

All eyes were fixed on Agamemnon, the tension thick in the air as they awaited his response.

"And how can I be certain that no one will strike me down during the duel?" Agamemnon inquired, his voice tinged with suspicion.

"They won't, you have my word." Achilles offered his assurance, his tone unwavering.

"I find myself less than convinced, young Prince. This savage creature does not inspire trust," Agamemnon retorted, increasing the pressure of his sword against Briseis's neck, a crimson trail of blood marking its path.

"She will not interfere," Achilles asserted with conviction, his gaze unwavering.

"And what makes you so certain?" Agamemnon questioned, skepticism lacing his tone.

"I have given my word. She will not intervene." Achilles reiterated, his voice carrying a weight of finality and resolve.

After a moment Agamemnon released his hold on Briseis and pushing her away from him.

A blend of fury and exasperation contorted Briseis's features as she directed her gaze towards Agamemnon. Retrieving Patroklos's spear from the ground, she strode over to Achilles with purpose.

"You could have easily killed him and ended this! Why are you doing this!? What are you trying to prove!?" Briseis's words erupted in a burst of emotion.

"I'm doing this for Patroklos," Achilles replied, his eyes holding her in a gaze filled with warmth and determination. "Trust me."

In a moment of tense silence, Briseis fixed her gaze upon Achilles, her emotions a turbulent mix of anger and conflict.Despite her seething frustration with Achilles for possibly allowing Agamemnon to evade an easy triumph, a realization began to dawn on her. Were it not for Achilles and Patroklos, she might have met her demise long ago. With a mixture of anger and gratitude, she forcefully took his hand and placed Patroklos's spear into it, signifying her acceptance as she left him to face his duel.

"You know, young Prince, it's rather amusing how effortlessly your ego can be manipulated. One would think you'd have outgrown such vulnerabilities by now," Agamemnon taunted, his words laced with derision.

The two warriors moved in a cautious dance around each other, their hands firmly clutching their weapons as they locked eyes.

"My motivations are not as you presume, 'King'," Achilles retorted. "I finally understand what I need to do, and you won't keep me from him."

"Sure, we'll see about that," Agamemnon retorted with a confident smirk, his eyes gleaming with determination.

Agamemnon wasted no time, launching into a relentless series of rapid attacks. Achilles intercepted the blows with his spear, but Agamemnon's strength prevailed as he seized the weapon, using it to draw Achilles in for a powerful headbutt.

The impact sent Achilles reeling backwards, momentarily disoriented. However, his warrior instincts quickly kicked in, allowing him to recover swiftly as Agamemnon pressed on with renewed aggression. Anticipating the next onslaught, Achilles skillfully evaded each strike with calculated precision, his movements fluid and precise, gradually wearing down Agamemnon through his strategic evasions.

As Agamemnon's onslaught gradually waned, Achilles keenly observed an opening for counterattack. With a graceful fluidity in his movements, he twirled his spear with finesse, the motion almost resembling a dance. It had been a while since he had moved with such agility, and a wave of nostalgia washed over him in that moment.

In the past, the sheer power of his spear had often sufficed, rendering such intricate footwork unnecessary. However, in this present confrontation, faced with a fair and evenly matched opponent, Achilles found himself reverting to the fighting style of his youth with an effortless ease that surprised even him.

Agamemnon strained to fend off Achilles's relentless assault, but the speed and precision of Achilles's strikes proved overwhelming. The swift movements of Achilles's spear left a trail of cuts on Agamemnon's arms, waist, and thighs, drawing blood with each precise hit.

Covered in his own blood, Agamemnon crumpled to the ground, defeated, his grip tightening on his grievous injuries.

Achilles declared, towering over his fallen adversary. "The battle is yours no longer. Return home." Achilles's voice resonated with finality as Agamemnon lay there, gasping for breath, defeated and humbled.

A sudden chuckle escaped Agamemnon's lips as he taunted, "Do you believe that sparing me will earn you a place in Elysium? You are weak... much like that boy of yours... the soldiers spoke of how he cried out for you as he lay wounded on the battlefield, a pitiful sight-"

Before Agamemnon could finish his cruel words, Achilles's rage surged forth, his hand closing around the king's throat in a vice-like grip, cutting off his words and his breath.

"Speak of him again, and I will rend you limb from limb," Achilles growled, his teeth clenched and eyes bulging. In his blinded wrath, Achilles unknowingly fell into Agamemnon's trap.

A sly smirk played across the King's face, as he swiftly drew a concealed dagger, catching Achilles off guard and driving the blade deep into the Prince's chest.

Achilles's eyes widened in shock, his mouth agape as he struggled to draw breath, the searing pain coursing through his body.

Releasing his grip on Agamemnon, Achilles staggered backwards, a desperate gasp escaping his lips as he summoned his spear with a flick of his wrist. As Agamemnon rose to his feet, Achilles hurled the spear with all his might, but his aim faltered, the weapon missing its mark. In a cruel twist of fate, Agamemnon stomped down on the dagger lodged in Achilles's chest, driving it deeper and piercing through his lung with a sickening finality.

Suddenly, Briseis emerged from the shadows, wielding Agamemnon's own sword as she drove it into his back with a bloodcurdling scream.

Agamemnon's scream pierced the air, a primal sound of agony and shock, as he attempted to elbow Briseis in a desperate bid for survival. However, to his dismay, she remained unfazed, clad in

Patroklos's formidable armor that rendered her impervious to his feeble attack.

In a chilling sequence of events, Paris emerged with his own sword, thrusting it mercilessly through Agamemnon's abdomen, the blade piercing through his guts with ruthless efficiency.

Agamemnon's hands instinctively grasped the weapon, his fingers slick with his own lifeblood as he futilely tried to wrench it free, each movement a testament to his waning strength and impending demise.

As the light of life dimmed in Agamemnon's eyes, a final, fatal blow came from King Priam, who drove his sword through Agamemnon's heart with a swift and decisive strike, bringing an end to the once-mighty king's reign of terror once and for all.

With the King's demise, a hollow emptiness settled within Briseis, a void where she had expected closure. Yet, as Agamemnon breathed his last, the world remained unchanged.

The anguished cries of the citizens reverberated through the air, the city engulfed in flames, the chaos unabated. The thirst for vengeance still burned within her, a relentless fire that refused to be quenched.

Struggling to compose herself amidst the turmoil, Briseis knew this was not the moment for reflection. Her gaze shifted to the fallen hero with golden locks, the one who had selflessly sacrificed himself for the greater good. His lifeless form lay motionless, a crimson river flowing from him like the eternal waters of Styx.

Briseis moved closer to the fallen hero, her steps heavy with sorrow as she knelt beside him, her hand gently clasping his in a gesture of reverence and disbelief.

"Why...why would you make such a foolish decision?" Her voice trembled with emotion, the weight of her words heavy with unspoken grief. "You could have won and kept your life! Why waste it like this?"

Her plea hung in the air, a desperate search for understanding in the face of his sacrifice. But the hero remained silent, his form still and unmoving, his gaze fixed on the twinkling stars above. And in that serene moment she noticed a faint, enigmatic smile upon his features.

As Briseis clasped his hand, a subtle weight caught her attention. Within his grasp lay a bracelet, its surface adorned with meticulously carved dice.

In that moment, a part of her understood that he could have easily killed Agamemnon at any moment, but that was not what he was fighting for.

Achilles' fight was one that would return him to his home, his philtatos, his agàpe.